Echoes of the Epoch
Stories and Poems

With compliments to Ananta & Piku

Kaushal
27/9/2019

Kaushal K. Srivastava

This book is a copyright material and must not be copied, reproduced, transferred, distributed, leased, licensed or publicly performed or used in any way except as specifically permitted in writing by the publishers, as allowed under the terms and conditions under which it was purchased or as strictly permitted by the applicable copyright laws. Any unauthorised distribution or use of this text may be a direct infringement of the author's or publisher's rights and those responsible may be liable in law accordingly.

ISBN-13: 9781791520717

Copyright © Kaushal K. Srivastava 2019

First published in 2019

For further information contact the author:
kkps1944@gmail.com

Available from
Amazon.com, Amazon.co.uk, Amazon.com.au, Amazon.in
and other online booksellers

Contents

Preface 5

Short Stories:
1. Floating City 7
2. Hidden Attraction 13
3. Life's Diary 38
4. Message of Midnight 91
5. Narrow Lane 102
6. New Destination 121
7. Turmoil in Heaven 141
8. Changing Values 153
9. Clever Man 158

Poems:
1. Air of Romance 165
2. Lessons of Life 167
3. We Live Together 169
4. Dilemma of Devotees 171
5. In Memory Lane 173
6. My Shadow Talks 175
7. Search for Global God 177
8. Cultural Garden 179
9. Flight No. 2017 181
10. Google's Kitchen 184
11. Digital Living 189
12. Buy One Get One Free 191
13. Where is Moonlight? 194
14. Death: A Perception 196
15. Poison of Corruption 197

Preface

Globalisation has changed the social structure of the Western world in recent decades. The unabated movement of people between continents has brought different cultures face to face, and an era of cultural confluence or cultural interface has emerged. This is euphemistically called multiculturalism, especially in the political parlance. In a sense, immigrants deeply rooted in one way of life have landed into a melting pot of conflicting ideas, norms, traditions, habits, and religious beliefs. Obviously, the society of the twenty-first century is rapidly evolving into a composite global village where competing values interact and adjust; and this has been the main theme of this book. Though the stories in this anthology are mostly centred on the interaction between Indian and Western outlooks, they may have universal implications as well. The savvy younger generation, prone to global aspirations, may see its own image in these writings. The poems on contemporary themes would also be interesting; some of them are satirical.

It would be desirable to say a few words about myself, which has a bearing on the framework of this book. As a physicist, I have worked in India, Australia, England, and the United States; and during this long journey I have observed many societal changes from a close distance. Post-retirement from Bhagalpur University, India, I have reflected on those changes and expressed them through my writings – short stories and poetry. The present title is an important link in that endeavor; my other books are listed at the end of this book.

Prof. Kaushal Kishore Srivastava
Melbourne, Australia.
Email: kkps1944@gmail.com

1. Floating City

The grandeur of a multi-storeyed luxurious cruise ship floating smoothly on blue waters of the Atlantic and the warmth of sunshine provided a rare combination to global tourists! 'What a beautiful weather' was on the lips of many when the ship left New York dock towards Florida. More than two thousand people of several nationalities had boarded the ship for a novel experience and enjoyment. It was summer time, schools and universities were closed, business had slowed down, and lots of people were on vacation – an annual ritual in the Western world. Families with young children, youths, couples, boys and girls, in casual dresses - sometimes scantly covered, roamed carelessly all over, as if they had got freedom for the first time. It presented the scene of a global village, often read in books but seldom seen so closely, where different cultures came face to face. Despite glaring differences in people's customs and manners, their co-existence and comradeship prevailed in the floating city. It appeared as if the boundaries between continents and political animosity among nations had disappeared for a few days, the whole world had contracted into a big mansion, and the physical existence of earth itself had evaporated. The vastly extended circle of horizon, the limitless expanse of blue waters, the turbulence of roaring waves, the invisibility of land mass, the twinkling clusters of stars in the night, the emerging crimson Sun at the distant horizon - all gave a unique feeling that was never realised in a city's life. *It was the empire of blue waters under the emptiness of blue sky – nothing existed apart from blue waters and blue sky!*

While the victory of technology over invincible oceans was worth celebration, it also reminded of the courage and life-threatening journeys undertaken by our ancestors who navigated in these waters in primitive boats and discovered landmasses that developed into the major centres of human civilisation. One often becomes philosophical when looking at the open sky and deep waters from the ship's deck, and the presence of humans seems like a negligible dot on the Nature's infinite canvass. But it is that very intelligent 'dot' in the universe which is the greatest miracle of creation.

In this floating city, Vikram, with a can of beer in his hand, was enjoying the pleasure of sunbath near a swimming pool. A book had fallen from his grip, perhaps he had become sleepy under the influence of alcohol. Helen was passing by, she picked up the book and looked at its title. Suddenly, Vikram became alert and said apologetically, "I don't know how the book fell from my hand. You can read it at your pace, I am not in hurry to take it back."

"The title of the book *New Acquaintance* is quite interesting. It has special appeal for those on the cruise – new people, new friends!" said Helen in a friendly voice.

"Do you like meeting new people? I feel hesitation – who knows how they react? In a sense, this world is shrinking as we are progressing towards economic globalisation, but the cultural and social separations do not seem lessening. In the past two days, you are the first person who has shown an interest in conversation with a stranger like me," said Vikram. Then he hurriedly put his T-shirt on thinking it was uncivilised to remain half-dressed before a young woman.

"The definition of etiquette changes near swimming pools, there was no need to hurriedly put on the T-shirt. Just see, I am also miserly dressed and the same can be seen around this place. What you did, could be good mannerism in your opinion but some people may regard it as a symbol of backwardness. This clash between life styles, which hardly catches our attention, may translate into social separation in due course, not because of any pre-conceived notion." Helen explained the situation carefully with a smile on her face.

"I am convinced at your logical reasonings. The reference mentioned by you is before my eyes – no further proof is needed." Vikram was amazed at her skilfulness.

She explained, "Differences in social dealings are natural, but they should not be construed arising from racial or sectarian attitudes. On this cruise, people have come from different countries and from myriad cultural backgrounds. Social globalisation lies in creating harmonious bridges between their customs and values, and gradually leading them to assimilate into the social mainstream. This will strengthen the on-going process of economic globalisation. Today, we need both."

"Not long ago, I had faced a similar situation but made a mistake in understanding its underlying meaning," said Vikram with a bit of remorse.

"Which event? Can I know?" Helen showed her curiosity.

"Before you say something, I would like to shelter myself from the bright sunlight – my body is already burning. White skinned people cannot tolerate strong sunrays, so I use a lotion on my body," she added.

"Let us take coffee in a restaurant. Any hesitation?"

"Why to distance from coffee? Coffee often becomes a link in fostering new acquaintance, there is a friendly touch in its fragrance." Both occupied a corner table in a dimly lit restaurant.

Vikram grabbed two cups of coffee. "Sugar and milk as per choice."

"How strange! We don't know each other's name, but we are talking and having coffee together. Isn't it so?" said Helen light-heartedly.

"My name is Vikram and I live in a township not far from New York. I feel uneasy in asking the name of an unknown young woman - you might say it is backwardness."

"Perhaps you got hurt from my earlier comment, but I had no such intention and I do apologise. I understand the gulf that exists between thinking and practical dealing, which is inherent in our personality." Sipping coffee, she spoke again, "How foolish I am – I lectured so much but did not tell you my name! I am Helen, and I study in a college in New York. This is the final year of my graduation and I work for a financial company on hourly basis. I have come on the cruise with my boyfriend – at this time he is doing workouts in the gym. Have you also come with your girlfriend?"

"Possibly, I could get one. Girlfriend is not a commodity that can be purchased from the market," said Vikram in a cheerful tone.

Helen burst into laughter, and quipped, "Well said – it appears you are expert in satires. I also enjoy jokes and satires, they immediately lessen the burden of mental stress. Remain alert – you may meet a girlfriend at the cruise itself!" Relishing her satirical reply, Vikram also could not help laughing. They were still sipping their coffee when Helen's boyfriend arrived. Helen introduced them, "This is my boyfriend John, and this is Vikram whom I met some time ago." John also bought a cup of coffee and joined them at the table.

Looking towards Vikram, Helen said, "Now tell us about that incident whose implications you could not comprehend properly. Perhaps, I can also learn something new."

"Maybe, it is laughable. That was my weakness - unfamiliarity with the new outlook."

"John intervened: "We belong to the same younger generation, open minded and outspoken. We can behave like friends and share our stories without reservation. Don't be too formal, Vikram."

Assured, Vikram narrated: "About six months ago, I took admission in a college for higher education and I am living with a family friend not far from New York. I come from a small-town middle-class family in India and I had no prior experience of living in a foreign country. It was the first day of my class, there were about a dozen students, when the Professor entered. I stood up – a mark of respect to the teacher - but no one else did that, and I heard some murmurs from the back bench. When I looked back, I saw that all were sitting comfortably; and they stared at me as if I came from an unknown civilisation! I was perturbed, and a bit ashamed too. Most probably, I was a victim of unspoken social discrimination.

"Realising the gravity of the situation, Professor Sahib said: 'local etiquettes or manners are bound to differ - they are not necessarily indicative of social or racial discrimination. If students born and brought up here go to a foreign country, they will come face-to-face with another culture rooted in unexpected values. In initial stages, one should remain cautious in reacting to local practices. Wherever there is a doubtful situation, there is no harm in asking others for guidance. In fact, not doing so could be a mistake with unintended consequences.'"

"What was the response of your classmates?" asked Helen sympathetically.

"When I explained that 'standing up' when a teacher enters the classroom is a symbol of respect in the Indian tradition, they appreciated it. Some of the classmates expressed their willingness to adopt this practice in their lives as well. I was moved by their response."

After listening attentively, John opined, "It is important to understand the face of the emerging multicultural society. From educational, economic, and scientific angles we are getting interconnected – effectively we are becoming global citizens - and this needs to be accepted in our day-to-day life. A global society needs a global culture, but it not easy to prescribe its parameters."

Helen almost gave a brief lecture: "Vikram, now you are living in America and, therefore, you should try to adopt the main elements of the local life-style. What constitutes the American way of life is difficult to describe in words, but that can be seen if you keep your eyes and mind open. That is present everywhere – in schools, universities, shopping centres, restaurants, public bars, swimming pools, and other public places – including this cruise ship. It does not mean that you completely disregard your heritage or traditions, rather it is quite unnatural to do so. How can one forget the history of one's life? Doing so might obliterate your identity and soil your dignity. One needs to adopt the middle path, which means leaving some of the old values and accepting some of the new ones. What to leave and what to accept depends on your wisdom, and that balance is subject to change with times. Newness is the chariot of progress, which includes embracing new values. How can one live in a society without being a part of its mainstream? This is called practical approach."

"Life's philosophy is hidden in your ideas, one has to ponder over them," Vikram said humbly.

They dispersed after a while. Helen noted down Vikram's phone number in her diary.

It was getting dark and stars were appearing in the sky. Soon, the full moon's silvery light reigned over the horizon and electric lights illuminated the ship. People were out on the open deck gossiping here and there; weather was pleasant; and the surrounding was joyful. Musical arenas, theatres, gambling counters, and other places of entertainment were agog with people. Restaurants and ice-cream parlours were getting crowded as well.

Vikram was alone, he finished his dinner early and came out of the restaurant. Holding a cup of coffee in his hand, he was watching the moon's image dancing in turbulent waters of the ocean. Just then, his phone rang: "I am Helen, where are you? Have you already taken your dinner? We didn't see you in the restaurant."

"Yes, I have taken my dinner. I didn't stay longer in the restaurant as I was alone."

"After an hour, a dance party will commence in the youth club. Can you come there? You can see some new faces and enjoy the party, you may share some drinks also."

"Coming to a dance party without a partner is uncivilised, and perhaps insulting too. You have John, but what will I do?" said Vikram in a disinterested tone.

"You are talking like a fool. There will be many men and women without a partner like you. One can find a companion from amongst them. Also, people often change partners and dance with them as a matter of social courtesy. I can dance with you, and so can John with other women. Then what short of hesitation? Enjoy the cruise, adopt new culture! I will wait for you." Vikram felt a magnetic attraction in what Helen said.

"Okay, I will join you there," he agreed.

The dance party continued till late in the night. Vikram danced with several women and consumed liquor intermittently. When he was dancing with Helen for the second time, his legs became unstable; the intoxication of alcohol had affected his movements. He almost fell into Helen's arms, when John rushed to support him. Vikarm was tired, he needed rest.

The next morning, after a peaceful sleep for several hours, he became almost normal. Feeling fresh after a warm shower, he wished to call Helen but hesitated. He was feeling a bit uncomfortable about what had happened last night – he did not know what to say. Unexpectedly, there was a knock on his door. "Who is there?" There was no reply. When he opened the door, he saw Helen.

"How are you feeling? Last night, you had come under the influence of alcohol."

"I had heard about telepathy, but today I am seeing it evidently. Only minutes earlier, I had wanted to call you but controlled myself – I didn't know how to face you. But my emotional waves touched you, and you are here! Thanks a lot for supporting me last night, and I do apologise for what happened," Vikarm said remorsefully.

"There is no need of thanks between friends. You might have done the same with someone else. If you are ready, we can go for breakfast." Saying so, Helen entered his room and spread the fragrance from her well-groomed hair.

"And John? Is he not coming?" inquired Vikram.

"He is still in bed, last night he consumed more Scotch than he could tolerate. The bad smell coming from his mouth did not allow me to have a sound sleep – I kept on changing sides on a sofa. After gulping two cups of strong coffee, I am feeling fresh. I have left a message on the table, hopefully he will join us for the breakfast." Both came to a restaurant on the deck. The glorious sunshine and cool air removed whatever little laziness was left in their body.

Eating a piece of omelette, Helen asked, "How was the last night's experience?"

"It was the first occasion for me. The party was exciting, spirited, and I fully enjoyed it. I was not sure of getting a partner at the dance party, but there were quite a few willing ones. You are an expert dancer, I might need a few lessons from you," said Vikram looking into her eyes.

"You may have to pay a fee."

"What fee between friends? If no thanks, then no fee!"

"You are skilful in conversation," she said jokingly.

She added, "This type of dance party is not only for entertainment, it has its social relevance as well. It provides a meeting platform to young men and women, where they can know each other and share their views. This opens a door for choosing life partners – not an easy task in the present stressful digital life. I also met John at one of these parties and soon we became friends. Maybe, you also find someone - keep your heart and mind open!"

"There is an emotional touch in your message; a memorable gift of this journey!"

"I hope we can meet occasionally after this cruise, we live in the same city." She uttered and got ready to go.

"Can I know your address?"

"Why not?" She pulled a card from her wallet and placed in his hand.

The midday approached soon. It was a hot and sweltering day; the swimming pool was crowded; and the management had planned a barbecue lunch around the pool in the Australian style. The variety of foods included international cuisines - Italian, Mexican, Indian, Chinese, Mediterranean – along with grilled sausages and drinks. As Vikram arrived late, he could not get a seat near the pool. Frustrated, he grabbed a can of cold drink and moved a short distance away. His eyes were fixed on the pool, as if he was looking for someone. Suddenly, he saw Helen and John playing with waters at the far end of the pool and was attracted towards them. He walked a few steps but stopped thinking: *It will be against the normal etiquette to disturb them in their moments of pleasure.* However, the reign of his wisdom loosened soon. Helen signalled him, and said, "Just come in the pool." At the same time, John said, "I have been here for almost two hours, and my intoxication has dissolved in the pool's water. I am feeling hungry and the smell of the barbecue is very inviting. You can join me for lunch."

"I had taken sumptuous breakfast, I might come later," replied Vikram.

Feeling shaky, Vikram entered the swimming pool. Earlier, he had swam several times with his college friends, but today's experience was thrilling - men and women were swimming together. They were playing a competitive game – Helen pulled him into her team. It was a unique scene of discipline and mutual respect between men and women, a social gift of the West. Vikram heard: 'You have a good control over balls, is your girlfriend also a good player?" When he looked around, a young woman volunteered, "Yes, I have said so. Both of you are invited for tomorrow's game, I like playing in waters."

Surprised, he said hastily, "You, who?" By that time, Helen had come out of the swimming pool.

"I am Sushma from New Jersey. I am on the cruise with my friend."

He was nonplussed, he didn't know what to say. The woman was beautiful and attractive – her eyes were agile, and her body was well maintained.

"Why are you gazing at me? Do I look like an alien? Did I say something wrong?" said Sushma, equally confused. Her tone was a bit harsh, but it was bathed in sweetness.

As if waking up from slumber, Vikram said meekly, "You have fired several questions, I don't know where to start from. Firstly, I would like to say that Helen, the woman I played with, is not my girlfriend – I met her on this ship itself. She is very sensitive and friendly in dealings, and she is here with her boyfriend. And you are not an alien, a woman of such pleasing personality can't be."

"And your name? Have you also come with your girlfriend? If yes, bring her tomorrow for swimming and the water game. If she doesn't know swimming, I can help her – she will like it." Sushma spoke uninterrupted.

"I am Vikram and I live in a place not far from New York. *It appears that no one is complete in America without a girlfriend or a boyfriend!* I have faced such questions earlier also. If I enquire about your boyfriend, how will you feel?"

"I would not mind. And I tell you that I have no boyfriend, because no one has passed the test."

"I praise your frankness. Would you tell me something about your so-called test?"

"Won't you leave it for another meeting? Let us meet in the restaurant at seven o'clock and ask Helen to join. I will book a table for dinner."

"Hopefully, the evening will be interesting," said Vikram with a smile.

The sun had already dipped below the horizon, but darkness had not fully descended. Vikram looked at his watch time and again, he was impatiently waiting for the appointed hour - seven o'clock. He paced his room thinking *whether the time had stopped moving forward!* He was eager to meet Sushma – her picture was before his eyes. When he reached the restaurant, he was received by Sushma who was present at the door with her friend. Then she introduced: "This is my intimate friend Priyatama; and this is Mr Vikram whom I met earlier in the day."

"Only Mr Vikram? Not even friend?" said Vikram sarcastically.

"This is the impatience in today's youths. They have devalued the word 'friend', like a cheap dress - you wear today and discard tomorrow." Vikram immediately realised that Sushma was matured, and she had intellectual depth behind youthful agility. He had not expected the conversation to start in this manner, he felt abashed.

Sushma also felt sorry at her harsh language. In a conciliatory tone, she said, "Vikram, I haven't made a personal comment on your mannerism – it was a general observation. If you were hurt, I apologise unreservedly. However, what I have said is like a bitter medicine – it burns your throat but purifies your body. I have also faced such odd moments."

"You have opened the window of truth in a few words. I know the truth is harsh, but it also provides the right guidance in our lives. Mutual friendship required a firm foundation, it cannot rest on a rosy platform made of sand," said Vikram thoughtfully.

Priyatama interrupted, "Both of you are busy in serious arguments, as if I am not present. Don't you think it is discourteous?" Just then, Helen and John entered the restaurant and were courteously received by Vikram. On his suggestion, they introduced themselves, shook hands with each other, and occupied the table already reserved.

Sipping a draught of wine, Vikram said, "Priyatama, I get nervous in calling you name. In Hindi language, the word 'Priyatama' is reserved for wife or intimate beloved. Its use will be the prerogative of a fortunate person and I don't want to deprive him from his right. I shall be calling you simply 'Priya' – any objection?"

A wave of laughter filled the air, the atmosphere became charged with friendly energy. Priyatama blushed, she had not expected such an analogy. Collecting her intellect, she replied, "Vikram, you are a hidden talent - you use literary language and throw colourful jokes. You may call me by any name, I won't mind. Whatever makes you happy is acceptable to me." Her response was measured and logical, and it was draped in sweetness. Vikram immediately realised that she was equally skilful and intelligent.

Helen protested, "Priyatama, this amounts to total surrender ignoring your personal choice. This is the era of women empowerment, younger generation is an important player in this social movement, and we need to safeguard its honour. Your submissive nature can bind you perpetually in emotional chains – it may adversely affect your family life."

"It is not surrender, it is generosity – the unique trait of womanhood. If Vikram gets satisfaction in calling me by any name – and if that does not hurt me – it is hardly objectionable."

Sushma intervened, "This may have a symbolic meaning for both sides. An indication of men's dominance and women's subjugation. In due course, it can take the form of women's exploitation – economic, social or physical. In this context, Helen's point of view is relevant and timely."

John, who was listening attentively, opined: "You people have started a debate on a controversial issue which has myriad dimensions. There are no fixed rules for judging women's exploitation or women's harassment; the whole basis is subjective especially when dealing with different cultures. Yes, I would like to say that objective differences in relationships should be duly respected – people can differ on certain issues even within a well-knit family. If women can get hurt, then why not men?"

Vikram broke the chain of arguments: "Let us stop further discussion on this topic, we have come on a cruise for enjoyment – not for unending vexed arguments. Now we should eat, and Priya can decide what to do after dinner."

"Very clever! Your way of appeasing Priyatama! Why this favouritism?" Sushma commented jokingly with a mystic smile.

"Sushma, do you remember your promise? I would like to know …"

Before Vikram could finish his sentence, Sushma quipped, "It is my personal matter, I will share it later. I never break my promise." She added, "Women, by nature, are more cautious in sharing their stories. But I will not disappoint you."

Priyatama suggested, "We can play cards after dinner. This might continue for two hours and we can take coffee in between." Helen and John left for a theatre after enjoying the tasty meal and others moved to Vikram's room which was spacious enough for three persons.

After half an hour, Sushma said, "Vikram, what's the matter? You are losing most of the games, it appears your attention is somewhere else."

"The remedy lies with you, try to recollect," responded Vikram.

"What a mystery? Both of you are talking in a symbolic language! I can leave the room for a while, if you want, so that you can talk freely," said Priyatama annoyingly.

Exasperated, Sushma explained: "Priyatama, there is nothing to hide from you. Okay, I will remove the suspicion – there is nothing mysterious. Vikram wants to know: *Why don't I have a boyfriend? What is my criterion for a boyfriend?* He waited for my answer at the dinner table itself, but I kept quiet in the presence of Helen and John because they come from a different cultural background than that of ours. In the American way of life, a boyfriend or a girlfriend is the urge of the youthful age that often includes sexual relationship. Several youths were also attracted towards me, but I asked one question: *Did you have a girlfriend earlier or do you have one now? Can you promise that no one will come between us?* No one ventured to make such a promise. A part of the Indian culture is still alive in me – that is, having only one sexual partner and a lifelong commitment to it. I am still waiting for a person who passes this test."

Thoughtfully, Priyatama said, "I am also deeply committed to this tradition and I fully support your contention. *In India, boys want virgin girls – then why not virgin boys?*"

Sushma hugged her out of jubilation. "You have raised the curtain in a few words – nothing more to be said." Vikram was amazed, he pondered if there was a message for him!

It was almost midnight, they said "Good night."

After two days. It was the last day of the cruise. John proposed, "Today's evening should be somewhat different and memorable." "You have snatched words from my mouth," said Vikram. They were taking coffee at a stall. "How about a champagne party?" "Provided we retain our senses."

Suddenly, Vikram thought of buying a gift and he proceeded towards the shopping arena. The dazzling markets of London and Paris were before him, but he could not decide what to buy. It was the first occasion when he wanted to buy a gift for a young woman. He had read in magazines that women have weakness for ornaments and cosmetics. Soon, he was before a counter selling expensive cosmetics made in France. He looked at various brands, but he could not decide what to purchase within his budget.

He heard a melodious voice: "Are you looking for something special? Can I help you?" This was the voice of a charming salesgirl.

"Cosmetics for gift," opined Vikram hesitatingly.

"For girlfriend or wife?"

"Again, the same ghost of girlfriend! Can't one live in America without it?" He said to himself in a whispering voice, but that was audible to nearby customers and they got startled.

"I do apologise. Did I say something absurd?" said the salesgirl apologetically.

"No, you don't have to apologise. In fact, I was engrossed in my own thoughts and I uttered something meaningless. It is I who should apologise for speaking loudly being unmindful of others' presence."

With a smile, the salesgirl spoke courteously, "Please decide from your heart, and let the mind rest for some time. This is the rule when buying cosmetics for loved ones."

Vikram could not help laughing. "You are perfectly right, and I hope to get the benefit of your experience. At this cruise itself, I have developed acquaintance with three young women - one has come with her boyfriend and I see the other two swimming alone in the pool."

"Give a book to the first one, and cosmetics to the other two. I can choose cosmetics for them."

"Okay, I like the idea."

Within a short time, the salesgirl brought two boxes of cosmetics and placed them before him.

"Why of different types?" enquired Vikram, surprisingly.

"Please take advantage of my expertise: one for the woman with smooth skin, and the other one for the woman with less smooth skin. Two faces are never the same, you must have got a chance to see them closely!"

Vikram came out of the shopping area pondering over the salesgirl's satirical statement.

The evening party was exciting. Sushma and Priyatama sang melodious songs, Vikram said jokes, John played on his mouth organ, and Helen recited a few love poems. They shared champagne and a variety of foods, danced together, and snapped photos in different poses. The party became a memorable event for all of them.

Delighted, Vikram said, "I have seen how friendly and open-minded women can be; and I have captured them in my camera. This way, I would be able to see your beautiful faces again. Any objection?"

"Have you also captured someone in your heart and mind?" quipped Helen.

"You will have to wait, time will tell. But one thing is certain – a new horizon has opened before my eyes and we all are within its perimeter."

"Long wait is not good, as the power of digestion gets weak." Priyatama commented satirically.

"Very true, your vision has become sharper," complemented Sushma looking into her eyes.

The party was to end soon, it was already past midnight. Vikram said *a small gift from me* and he placed three packets on the table – one each for Helen, Sushma, and Priyatama.

"Can we open our packets?"

"Yes, why not?" Vikram was also anxious to know their reaction.

Helen jumped with joy seeing the book *New Acquaintance*. "It was this very book which brought us together – it is precious for me. Thanks a lot for your thoughtful gift."

Sushma and Priyatama spoke at the same time, "Such an expensive gift! How can we repay?"

Vikram said in a low voice, "Just a sweet smile!"

"In the last four-five days only, you have become romantic. Congratulations for adopting the American way of life! I have read about cross-cultural living in a global village, but I never had a chance to absorb its real meaning. Today, I celebrate it!" Helen became ecstatic and kissed Vikram's hand affectionately.

They spoke in one voice: Cheers!

2. Hidden Attraction

"May I come in, Sir?"

"Why? What's the matter? Why are you so late today?" Dr Prabhat Sharma asked interrupting his lecture. Dr Sharma was a senior teacher in the psychology department of the college who had earned his doctorate from a foreign university only two years ago. He looked smart, younger than his actual age when dressed in jeans and shirt. He was praised for his scholarship and dedication to work, and he was very punctual as well. Coming to class and leaving it on time had become a part of his nature, and he expected the same from students.

Hesitatingly, Sudha said, "I had left home for the college in time, but my rickshaw remained stranded on the road because of a long procession lead by a political party. I have learnt the value of time from you itself, but I was helpless." Her polite voice and innocence were so persuasive that the entire class supported her by thumping the desk.

Judging the mood of the students, Dr Sharma permitted Sudha to come into the class; any sign of reluctance was not visible on his face. She came hastily and occupied a seat on the nearest front bench along with other boys, though she used to sit on an ear-marked side bench along with three-four other girls. By then, almost half of the time was already gone and soon the bell rang announcing the end of the period. While leaving the class, Dr Sharma told her, "The first part of the lecture had many important ideas, you may take its brief write-up from me at the lunchtime." Someone from the rear bench sounded a whistle! Another voice was heard, "This is just the first meeting!" Sudha was not perturbed, she was aware of such unusual teasing jokes in the college, often targeting girls. They were much less crude than the hurtful ragging often prevalent in many cosmopolitan colleges.

Sudha was studious and a symbol of humility, her civilized manners had added a layer of attraction on her limited beauty.

People often looked at her with piercing eyes, but with no ill meaning; she was admired for her simplicity and traditional inexpensive costumes. She was knocking at the door of adolescence - not far away from blooming with full glow. Her big eyes had natural attraction, she kept away from artificial expensive make-ups.

Lunchtime arrived, the campus buzzed with activities. Hordes of boys and girls marched towards the college canteen, laughing and jostling, and Sudha was one of them. Many teachers were also out for food and drink. She finished her lunch quickly and walked towards Dr Sharma's office. Soon she knocked at his partially a-jar door.

"Yes, come in. Why were you so late? I was rather waiting for you."

"I am sorry that you had to wait. I had thought that you were also taking lunch somewhere. The fire of hunger can engulf wisdom, one should keep away from it. The great rishis have also said *one cannot pray empty-stomach*, then teaching could be much more difficult when hungry."

"The fire of hunger burns the body, whereas heart's fire can consume thoughts. The fire of hunger can be extinguished in a canteen, but how can one win over the heart's fire? In other words, how can one quench the fire of thoughts? Have you ever considered?"

Sudha responded thoughtfully, "I could not comprehend what you said. What is heart's fire? Does it have any direct manifestation? It is not possible to comment on your queries without delving deep into these obscure matters." There was surprise in her eyes.

"This is the field of psychology – analysis of mind, study of emotions, conceiving thought processes, identifying mental waves, etc. The seeds of affection, love, and intimacy germinate from those invisible mental waves, and they bestow meaningfulness to human lives. Without them, humans may not be much different from stones." Dr Sharma spoke uninterrupted.

Sudha got overwhelmed by his forceful statement, she was mesmerised by the magnetic attraction of his scholarship. His articulation was short but loaded with challenging ideas, especially for a young college student. She was thrilled, she stood motionless like a statue. She became alert when she heard, "Which world are you lost in?"

"I am alright. I just got trapped in my own thoughts," she replied meekly.

"You will get more occasions in future to ponder over these aspects. Keep these hand-written pages which describe the summary of my lecture. You can return them after a few days."

"Yes, Sir." She grabbed those pages and walked away slowly, as if half-asleep.

Once at home, she engrossed herself into those pages.

"The study of human relationship is an important domain of psychology. Its practical side is equally useful: social stress and emotional conflict in relationships are becoming a common sight, and they have increased the demand for professional psychologists. To ensure social stability by providing right counselling to mentally depressed people is considered an obligation for trained psychologists. At the same time, it is deceptive to consider psychology as a proven experimental science because there is no instrument to measure emotional aberrations. It is a matter of experience and therefore personal foresight is a commendable asset."

"Those who worship vibrant youthfulness, enchanting beauty and emotional indulgence are usually governed by their heart, rather than thoughtful mind. As a result, they feel frustrated when reality does not conform to their expectations. They often develop pessimistic attitudes full of bitterness and the world looks dark for them."

"A woman can err in assessing intimate love because of sentimental weakness, but she does no mistake in recognising disinterestedness or neglect. This instinct of a woman is her greatest moral strength and her reliable companion as well."

"The line of demarcation between ideal love and sexual urge is blurred, and youthful eyes often fail to see it. Study brings maturity in thinking, opens the windows of wisdom, and makes life enjoyable in a real sense."

Reading this much in one seating made Sudha's ears warm - as if all membranes of her brain had become active and they were radiating energy. To visualise the philosophy of whole life in a few words was a novel experience for her, she became ecstatic. She was overwhelmed by the magnetic attraction of these words, and she felt a strange sensation. She closed her eyes, she would read them again the next day.

At the breakfast table, she opened those pages again and read them inquisitively so that she could prepare herself for the next class. Suddenly, she saw a hand-drawn picture on the last page. Though it was not well sketched or easily identifiable, its features resembled the face of a young woman. It seemed the person, who drew this picture, was in a haste or perhaps it was his first attempt. She reasoned: *The write-up belonged to Dr Sharma, who else could have drawn that picture?* A lightening thought came into her mind: *Was it her picture?* She trembled with unknown fears! Human mind is very suspicious - once an apprehension enters the mind, it is hard to get rid of it. Sudha was also not an exception.

When she came to return those pages, Dr Sharma was on leave. After a few thoughtful moments, she wrote a line below that picture: "Could not understand the picture's message." Then she put those pages in a sealed-envelope and dropped it in his letter box.

After many days, it was Dr Sharma's lecture she was anxiously waiting for. He surveyed the class and said: "To understand the language of pictures is also an important art in psychology. One can assess the mental state of a person by reading his or her face and construct a picture of the underlying feelings that could be related to sadness, happiness or just emptiness. This is often known as body-language, in a simple sense, which does have relevance for practicing psychologists.

Similarly, pictures can serve as a complementary language, especially when there is hesitation in talking face-to-face."

Intelligently, Sudha questioned, "If the picture is blurred or unidentifiable, how can one derive any meaning out of it? In such a situation it would be useless to peek under its hidden message, if any."

Someone from the back bench intervened, "Sir, I can sketch two pictures of your appearance: in one you will look like a well-groomed jolly professor, but a crooked person in the second one. They will create entirely opposite impressions - how can they be relied upon?" The class burst into laughter at this jocular comment.

Within no time the class became attentive again. Dr Sharma continued his discourse with seriousness: "There is a contradiction in your observation. You will sketch my picture as per your experience and inner voice. Yes, you can do anything for monetary gains, but for that you will have to mortgage your ethical values. Pictures are like living objects, they radiate invisible waves that touch the hearts of onlookers. A painter or sculpture loves his creation, talks with it in an unspoken language, and gets emotional satisfaction. If you get a chance, talk to them."

Then he turned towards Sudha and explained, "What you have said is quite natural, but think why a picture looks blurred or vague. When we see a person or an object casually, we hardly fix their image in our mind. Pictures drawn on that basis will lack clarity and depth. This also applies to studies, relationships, and other dimensions of human activities. However, a closer and continued interest in the subject can sharpen those pictures and make them attractive too. Such pictures create an unseen, unspoken, bond between the creator and the object."

Sudha became almost certain that the background of today's lecture was that very picture and her comment written underneath. Why so? Dr Sharma could have ignored this topic and elucidated other aspects of his last lecture as contained in his write-up, in fact those ideas were more challenging. Why so much emphasis on pictures? What does it indicate? The same question again arose in her mind: W*as it her picture?* It was difficult to be sure, it could be someone's else. She will have to wait, perhaps the vagueness gets replaced by clarity next time! He had also said: '*A painter loves his creation.*' What does it mean? Has he fallen in love with this undefined woman, whoever she is? She was perplexed, she fell asleep arguing with herself.

Almost for a month Dr Sharma did not talk about the relevance of pictures in his lectures, though he did not forget to throw a casual glance on Sudha whenever possible. There was nothing unusual in his gesture, and she was also relieved. Naturally, she had in effect forgotten the picture's episode and was able to concentrate on her studies.

Today, Dr Sharma's lecture's topic was "key to success." He said, "The definition of success is complex, it has myriad dimensions, it has no objective criterion, and there is no single measuring technique. In fact, it is a matter of personal realisation, a product of emotional intelligence. A colourful flower is the symbol of love for many, whereas it is merely a natural stage in the life cycle of plants for scientific observers. Many people consider earning adequate money as the key to success, whereas few others regard academic achievements." A touch of scholarship was evident in his observations; it was one of his most impressive lectures.

An inquisitive student asked, "Does psychology play any role in this decision?"

"It is a very relevant question. All of you write a brief note on this topic and submit it to my office by the next week," told Dr Sharma. "Consider it as a project, your answer should be well-thought and logical."

Sudha intervened, "Is it not true that the basis for measuring success changes with time? Is it not affected by the dynamics of life?" The excitement at her face did not go unnoticed.

"Certainly, nothing is absolute or static in time-frame. You may elucidate these points in your presentation," said Dr Sharma looking straight into her eyes.

The week passed like a flying bird. Dr Sharma, sitting in his office, was examining the papers submitted by the students. The views expressed by them were on the following diverse lines:

"Wealth is most important for success in life."

"Social prestige is the corner stone of success."

"Becoming a celebrity in any field is the key to success, whatever be the means."

"Success is a mirage, it is difficult to catch. Like a dream, it has no objective basis."

"Success comes from social recognition, whereas psychology is a part of mental training. I hardly see any relation between the two."

Finally, he read the write-up submitted by Sudha. "Success lies in the fulfilment of desires. As desires germinate in mind, success and psychological processes are interlinked but often unseen. Desires change and therefore success is a slave of time. In student life success comes through earning knowledge; but in the youthful age one craves for intimate love and its realisation is the key to success. What happens in the distant future is just a conjecture, whereas the concept of success lives in the present." At the end she had drawn the picture of a young man whose face was partially covered with hanging dark hair, but his bright blue tie was clearly attractive.

Dr Sharma's eyes got fixed on that picture: *Whose picture was it?* Does she want to convey some message? He looked at the picture time and again trying to recognise the sketchy face but could not succeed. Suddenly, he was attracted to the 'bright blue tie' – was it a silent signal of something? He could not decipher.

He was not seen in the campus for the next two weeks. As Sudha was eager to know about her presentation, she went to his office and knocked at the partially opened door, but there was no reply. Reluctantly, she entered the empty room and saw some loose papers lying on the table. Unexpectedly, a gust of air threw those papers on the ground, which she collected and arranged on the table. Surprisingly, on one of the sheets she saw a picture resembling her face and thought: *Is Dr Sharma really attracted towards her?* She stood motionless for a few minutes like a statue and kept on pondering. Impulsively, she put that sheet in her bag and walked away in a pensive mood.

The very next week, it was the semester's last class that would be followed by one month's vacation. A blue tie was shining on Dr Sharma's white shirt and there was a thick packet in his hand. He told the students, "I have read your write-ups and given my comments. If you have questions in this regard, you can see me after the vacation." He distributed the papers among them and appeared relaxed. "There will be no formal lecture today, but we can interact informally."

Looking serious, a student said, "Sir, I have seen you in many attires, but your tie's colour is always blue. Is there a mystery in this? Does it indicate the rigidity in your viewpoints? A reluctance towards change? Or is there a silent message in this?"

Sudha sprang to her feet, saying with a tinge of sarcasm: "My friend, you have rather snatched my words. The language of attires can be understood by a scholarly psychologist only!"

At once, a flash of light shone in Dr Sharma's mind. He looked at her with piercing eyes and said to himself: s*he has also become expert in the sign language.* Momentarily, a smile appeared on his lips. Then, looking towards that student, he explained, "Your investigative spirit is laudable. You can derive any meaning, but that may not be necessarily true. The 'silent language' can only be a complementary medium, it cannot take the place of a lively language. Hence, one should exercise caution in arriving at any conclusion."

After classes were over, Sudha stepped into his office unannounced. He was puzzled: "What's the matter? Any special reason?"

"Perhaps, this sheet of paper belongs to you." She placed it on his table.

"Where did you get it? I was anxiously looking for it." He felt relieved.

"Out of curiosity, I came here to see your comments on my essay, but you were not available. Several sheets lying on your table got scattered by a sudden gust of wind, and I found this one by chance. Naturally, it is your property and hence I have come to return it. I apologise that I had entered your office in your absence." She said politely.

"You have rightly said that it is my property. A sheet of paper has no monetary value, but my emotions are embedded in this picture. That makes it a valuable property."

"But this picture is unfinished," she remarked.

"It is simply imaginative at this stage, it needs filling with colours. I am not sure which colours to use." With some hesitation, he spoke again: "You have also drawn a picture at the end of your essay, but its message is not clear. Dress it with colours, give it life."

"Really? Why can't we see both the pictures together when they are ready?"

"This advice is credible. Psychology also says that pictures have their own language, maybe our joint effort translates into an educational experiment!" Dr Sharma spoke in a contemplative tone with no trace of excitement.

The college was closed for the vacation and Dr Sharma had also gone away. Winning over the initial inertia, Sudha grabbed a brush for filling the picture with the *colour of love*, but her fingers declined to move. A wave of wisdom alerted her: "Is it the intoxication of youthfulness? Or just foolishness? Have you considered its consequences? What if he doesn't accept your *flower of love*? What happens if someone else resides in his mind? Or his thinking is different? This situation can be calamitous for both of you." An alarm sounded from within, "Remember his warning: *The line of demarcation between ideal love and sexual urge is blurred.* Then, why this transgression in a hurry?" She became fearful and decided to wait.

On the other side, Dr Sharma was thinking of the conversation he had when she came to return his paper. He reasoned with himself: *She was intelligent enough to recognise her picture, though it was not clear. That's the reason she proposed to see the two pictures together, sketched by each of us. In a way, it is also the test of my intentions.*

The college opened after the month-long vacation, but Dr Sharma was not seen for several days. When he didn't turn up for two weeks, Sudha enquired from the college office and learnt that he had gone abroad to participate in a seminar. She felt some indignation, "Did he forget the context of the pictures? How careless?"

After a long absence, Dr Sharma surfaced in the class. The topic of his lecture was "an aspect of human relations". Like a consummate scholar, he argued: "Attraction or imaginative love is the product of a mental state, which gives pleasure to a person even when lonely - just like poetry, painting or melodious songs. Assuming it as the reality of life could be a mistake, but it is also true that hidden attraction is often the first step on the ladder of satisfying love. Hence, it is desirable to give the relationship enough time to mature, just as a tender bud takes time to blossom into a beautiful flower. The consent of both heart and mind is very important in human relationships." He glanced at the attentive class, and spoke again, "If you happen to work as a professional psychologist, you will find many occasions to counsel on complex problems related to intimate relationships between partners. As prudent professionals, you should be conscious of these matters in your life as well."

Breaking the silence of the class, a student asked, "You might have heard of *love at first sight*, is it false?"

"It happens in films only. I consider it an exception in real life," said Dr Sharma promptly. Sudha asked curiously, "How much time is sufficient? Any estimate?"

With a smile on his lips, he replied: "Love is not a simple plant which has a fixed season or time for flowering and giving fruits. It is an *emotional plant* which germinates and grows on the heart's soil. *When it matures or when it will wither* is unpredictable, unfathomable. It must be remembered that misdemeanour has no place in the game of attraction, it must have the cover of time-tested social morality."

Sudha immediately realised that under the pretext of lecturing on imaginative attraction and its psychological implications, Dr Sharma had unveiled his own feelings. He considers pictures as tender plants and there is depth in his arguments. She was again overwhelmed by his scholarship and practical approach. Mentally, she firmed up, undertook a resolution and smiled. She would be playing her cards more cautiously and less impulsively.

Several months passed. She did not miss a chance to say 'hello' whenever she saw him, and in return he also responded with a thin smile. Examinations were coming close and all classes had formally ended. The golden period of the college life will be over in the next two-three months, and life will take a new turn thereafter. In the meantime, 'Teachers' Day' was to be celebrated in the college. In the great Indian tradition, teachers are regarded as builders of society, they are supposed to lay the foundation of morality and wisdom in students, and in return they are highly respected. On this day, a function, attended by teachers and students, was held in the college auditorium. Many students paid glowing tributes to teachers and thanked them for their guidance. When Sudha got a chance, she said in an emotive tone:

"In books, I have read the history of knowledge and science
In lectures, I have heard the scholars' deliberations
In pictures, I have seen the future's dream
In heart, I have saved a lively imagination.
I convey Teachers' Day greetings with jubilation
It is heavy on heart - at this moment of separation."

She became emotional, her voice almost choked. She said the last sentence facing Dr Sharma who was seated in the front row. He also felt the pain of these words.

While returning home, she knocked at his door. "Who?" "I am Sudha, can I see you for two minutes?" Entering his office, she said, "A small gift for you."

"I don't accept any gift from students, it is not consistent with my work culture."

"Today, it is my right – it's Teachers' Day," said Sudha with humility.

Dr Sharma became disarmed at this reply. He kept the packet: "What's inside?"

"You can open it."

There was a beautiful tie of blue colour. "I will definitely wear it."

The very next day, he saw the letter 'S' woven in silk threads on the back side of the tie.

The exams were due to start in two-week's time. Many students of psychology arrived in Dr Sharma's office to take advice on some expected topics, and Sudha was one of them. She felt satisfied that he was wearing the tie gifted by her. Finally, a student expressed his desire to work with him after the results were out. "Perhaps, I won't be available as I am going abroad for one year," said Dr Sharma.

Sudha felt an internal jolt, "Is it my second examination?"

The students were coming out of his room and Sudha was last in the line. She heard Dr Sharma's mild voice, "The colours of the silk threads are attractive." This much indication was enough for her, she was elated.

Time passed quickly. Sudha passed her exams with flying colours, she was looking for a professional job, and she had already contacted a few practicing psychologists. Unexpectedly, she received a message from Dr Sharma: "I am leaving by a flight at 3 o'clock." It was already late morning, she was astonished and angered: "Why such insensitivity? Attraction and unkindness at the same time? What short of relationship is this?" But her insight cautioned her: "He might not have intimated you, had he not felt the bond of attraction. This is unspoken attraction. Give it time to flourish, he had also said so in his lecture."

At the airport, she met him with a bouquet of roses but was surprised that none else from the college was there to see him off. In a soft voice, he told her, "It is desirable that our feelings are not exhibited in the open, that may become a fodder for mischievous minds. Emotional waves are powerful, they reach their destination per se. I have purchased this magazine, you are mature enough to read it." He left for boarding the plane.

Sudha was in her bedroom. While looking at the magazine's coloured pages, she was attracted to an article *love is a trade*. "Love is like a trade, which is based on the principle of give-and-take. The so-called ideal love, where there is nothing to exchange, is just an imagination. It is impractical, unrealistic, and short-lived. Talent, goodness, and beauty cannot be shared or bartered, though their powerful effects can be realised. If girls want to love someone, what can they offer? The same question applies to boys. The only thing they can share is their body. This is called sex in a crude language. But this is the bitter reality and the basis for a fruitful life." Momentarily, for the first time, she was gripped with sexual excitement! She became restless and could not sleep well.

In the morning, she pondered over the entire matter with a clear mind: "Dr Sharma must have read this article, then what was the purpose of advising me to read it? He had also said *you have become mature,* what does it mean? Does he want to establish sexual relationship with me? But he is a great believer in social decorum, and he would never trespass that boundary. Hence, it points to only one logical conclusion – he wants to make me his life partner. His proposal in contained in this article itself; and I have to take the final decision." She looked at the beautiful sky, smiled, and took a flight of imagination!

Very soon, Sudha joined a group of practicing psychologists. She counselled many young lovers who were trapped in sexual relationships in the early years of their lives and had become dissatisfied within a short time. They had lost the initial warmth of the intimate love, they were frustrated, separated, and looking for a new beginning. The lessons taught by Dr Sharma were vividly before her, she thanked him for sharing his prudence.

After one year. Dr Sharma and Sudha were taking dinner in a restaurant. Suddenly, he placed a book titled *Hidden Attraction* in her hands saying: "A gift for you. I wrote this book during my stay abroad." As she opened the book, she saw 'Dedicated to Sudha Sinha' printed in bold.

"Who is this Sudha Sinha?" She asked surprisingly.

"She is sitting in front of me," said Dr Sharma in a dignified tone.

In the book's preface, he had written, "Sudha Sinha was my student. It is by her inspiration that I could do an experiment on the relevance and effectiveness of pictures in the field of psychology. I am greatly indebted to her."

"Have you considered me just a resource material for conducting an experiment?" She spoke with pain and annoyance.

"I consider the whole life as an animated laboratory! Both of us are its actors, look at its positive side. This book has bonded us together."

Sudha was trying to digest the depth of his statement.

While she was still in a pensive mood, Dr Sharma placed a picture on the table saying: *I keep my inspiration with me.* It was a beautiful hand-drawn picture of Sudha filled with the *colour of love.*

She was amazed, she became sentimental. Controlling her emotions, she opened her handbag, picked up a picture, and placed it on the table. It was Dr Sharma's picture with an attractive blue tie.

Placing both the pictures side by side, he told her: "These two are complementary. Once you had said 'Why can't we see our hand-drawn pictures together?' That desire has been fulfilled today."

Sudha kept on watching those pictures, she was in a dreamland.

Dr Sharma kissed her hand, but she did not protest.

It was the first occasion that he touched her, she felt a warm sensation. At once, she exclaimed: "Now you are not Dr Sharma, but simply Prabhat. I am blessed!"

3. Life's Diary

"Mango chutney is very tasty, can I have more?"

The tone was loud, but sweet. Sanjay was taking dinner with two-three friends in a restaurant, his unconscious mind felt an impulse of attraction – as if a forgotten memory came alive momentarily. He looked around trying to find where the voice came from, but that proved futile in the din and bustle of the busy restaurant on a Saturday evening. That voice seemed familiar to him, but almost forgotten. His mind started rewinding swiftly the blurred images of the past hoping to find a live thread. But soon he became busy in chitchats with his friends.

After some time, he heard "a glass of water, please" in the same voice that penetrated deep into his mind; he quickly turned around and sensed that the voice came from a corner table which was occupied by a few ladies who were more likely to be accepted as young women. It was difficult to know whose voice it was; he had no option but to keep conversing with friends – albeit in somewhat absent-minded manner. His curiosity had not died, he kept looking towards that table.

On weekends, Indian restaurants in Melbourne are usually crowded and this one was not an exception. Spicy foods are considered beneficial to health and they attract many foreigners to Indian restaurants – spicy food and Indian culture go together. Sanjay had joined the queue for making payment; he saw that one of those ladies came behind him and others waited outside the door. As he came out, his eyes suddenly fell on those ladies and an image appeared in his mind like a flash of lightening. One of them looked familiar, but he could not be sure because of a thick layer of cosmetics on her face and curly hair style. He moved towards her with a question on his lips, but he restrained himself – perhaps it would be awkward. He self-debated: *Did the lady see him? Could she recognise him? Am I mistaken?*

Standing at a short distance, he was trying to light a cigarette when he heard: "Have you come from Hyderabad?" It was the same sweet voice which he had heard in the restaurant. Surprised, he saw a young woman facing him.

"Yes, I have. But any special reason for your question? Why did you guess so?"

"I recognise you. You were my classmate, and more than once we had said *namaste* to each other. You haven't changed much over the years and therefore it was not difficult to identify you." She said courteously, though amazed at this sudden meeting.

With equal humility, Sanjay replied: "I could sense the sweetness of an old acquaintance when I heard your voice in the restaurant, and since then I have been trying to recall who she was. Your face seemed a bit familiar, but I could not be certain about its identity. I wanted to talk to you, but hesitated – rather I felt shy. Now I am on a firm footing."

"How sweet! The impression of my voice still resides in your mind! Do you remember my name?"

"Why not? You are Sangita Verma - your voice complements your name. In fact, your lyrical voice is your real identity! Perhaps, you might have forgotten – my name is Sanjay."

Sangita quipped, "Girls have sharp memory! You are Sanjay Arora, and you were a member of the college cricket team." A thin smile appeared on her lips.

In the meantime, her friend came from the restaurant and they got ready to leave. Hurriedly, Sanjay pronounced, "Next Saturday, I will come here again. And I will wait for you."

The history of her own pleasing life, when she was a college student, became alive in her sleepy mind. She was agile, sociable, and known for melodious singing; she had won prizes in the college for her entertaining performances. She was not rich in beauty, but there was a natural attraction in her big eyes; and her voice was melded in sweetness. After leaving the college, a sudden change came into her life which brought her

to Melbourne. She pondered: "If Sanjay asked about her welfare, what would she say? He was a classmate like many others - their occasional interaction never went beyond hello or formal greetings. She did not know much about him except that he was foremost in studies – several of his articles were published in college magazine – and he played good cricket."
On the other hand, Sanjay's state of mind was not much different; he hardly knew much about Sangita. He reasoned: "Did he commit a mistake by expressing his desire to meet her again at the restaurant? How did she take it? Had he known her phone number, he could have apologised for this impertinence. Not going to the restaurant could be doubly foolish!" He felt helpless, he decided to take a chance.

The appointed day came sooner than expected. Sangita was in a predicament – should she go to the restaurant? Had she known Sanjay's phone number, she could have evaded it earlier on some pretext, but doing so now would be considered uncivilised. It was she who had started the conversation, it was her responsibility to keep its honour. She decided to go and remain cautious in dealing with him.
 The evening sky was getting reddish, it was time to get ready for the dinner. Sangita stood before a big mirror, chose her cosmetics and matching dress carefully that added to her natural attraction. At the restaurant's gate, she was welcomed by Sanjay. "You are looking smart."
 "Thanks." Sangita accepted the compliment with a smile.
 They occupied a table, booked in advance by Sanjay. Hesitatingly, he asked, "Would you mind having wine? Or the usual soft drink?"
 "As you like."
 Soon they were served red wine and some savouries. Sanjay was not sure how to start the conversation - which topic to choose. He broke the silence, "How do you find Melbourne's variable weather – four seasons in one day?" Sangita understood his dilemma, she smiled and replied: "We are here

not to discuss the weather; I presume you are a bit nervous in asking any personal question but that is what you want. Prior to this, we had never sat together even for a cup of coffee and hence your hesitation is natural. Therefore, I would like to make our path easy by talking about myself."

She continued, "I got married three years ago, but I am living alone in Melbourne for the past two years. My ex-husband lives somewhere else in this country itself, but I don't know where. I work in a supermarket - three to four days per week - and live with a woman-friend."

"Ex-husband?" Sanjay was puzzled.

"Within a year of our marriage, we started living separately. A few months ago, our divorce petition was approved by the court. I can't tell you why it happened, and how it happened." She became emotional, her eyes became wet.

"I don't want to reopen your psychological wounds; my sympathies are with you."

They remained silent while sipping wine from their glasses; they were digesting the depth of the ugly situation. Soon the waitress came to take orders for the main course.

Looking at the menu card, Sanjay asked her, "Any special choice? Veg or non-veg?"

"Your choice will be fine for me also, I have no restriction."

He placed orders for a few dishes - veg and non-veg both. The waitress informed them that it could take half-hour before the dinner was served - not unusual on a Saturday evening. Regaining her composure, Sangita spoke in a soft voice 'it's your turn to share your experiences'.

Gulping a piece of kebab, Sanjay said: "I was waiting for you to feel comfortable, lest my situation might add to your agony. I am an IT professional living here for the past four years; I got married about three years ago. We feel satisfied; we love each other; but my wife does not like to live here – she feels isolated from the cultural and social traditions of this country. The machine-like life style of the Western society irritates her, and she feels dejected internally. She has already made three-four long visits to Hyderabad in recent years, and presently she is there. Loneliness bites me – the downward path is often slippery!"

Looking into her eyes, he added, "Now I understand why friendship is so valued in this country; friendly chitchats can reduce mental burden and show new lights. Perhaps, both of us need it."

"You may come out of this agonising situation in a simple way: just go back to Hyderabad – you can easily find a professional job there – and live happily with your wife and other relatives. It is not advisable to sacrifice family life at the altar of material comforts in a distant world. No friendship can take the place of a wife – this realisation becomes more powerful with growing age." Sangita spoke with conviction.

"It is easier said than done. This solution is easy to propose, but difficult to accept in real life. Professionally, I feel satisfied here and the challenge of working in a global environment is intellectually inspiring. If I go back to where I came from, my talent may get stunted due to restrictive processes in the world of business. It is often heard: the youthful years are most congenial for the talent's evolution, one harvests its benefits in the future."

"Your perspective describes one sides of the situation, but there could be other dimensions. *The two sides of a river never meet, but they are needed for the river's disciplined flow.* Similarly, you should also try to find an acceptable path."

Smilingly, Sanjay observed: "Your literary language is praiseworthy. Words are few, but they send a powerful message."

Soon dinner was served at their table, the fragrance spreading from the dishes was inviting. Relishing some of the items, Sangita admired his choice and enquired, "Do you come here very often?"

"There is hardly any other option. When my wife is away, I come late from the office and don't like to cook. In fact, the Indian cooking is cumbersome for anyone."

"Eating out very often is not good for health. If you approve, I can cook for you once in a week at my home and you can pick up at your convenience. That way, you can eat homemade food at least a few times in the week." She said hesitatingly.

"Thanks for your offer. Would you like having one more serve of wine?"

"No, not now. Maybe on some other day." She said casually.

Sanjay thought it was a signal for meeting again, he felt elated. Sangita picked up her bag: let's go, it is getting late.

"A little while more – just for coffee," urged Sanjay. She could not deny.

Sipping a draught of coffee, Sanjay told her, "I have no intention to intrude into your privacy, but I would like to ask you a question."

"If that is what you want, I won't disappoint you. But it is not necessary that I should reply."

"Was your marriage arranged? Or was it a love marriage?" He fixed his eyes on Sangita.

She was puzzled at this unexpected question, she was rather alarmed, and remained quiet for some time in a thoughtful state. Taking a long breath, she replied, "You are testing my patience, forcing me to take a tough examination. I can't tell a lie and the truth is ludicrous. Promise me that this matter will remain between two of us only."

"You can confide in me; I won't betray your trust."

"My marriage was arranged - not by my parents but by Google! I came into touch with someone on Facebook; he talked lovingly, seemed well educated, promised heavenly love, and what not. I became mad in his love and hypnotised by his charm. My parents tried their best to dissuade me from such characters - who could be dubious – but I did not yield. Frustrated by my obstinacy, they gave permission for our marriage. The guy came to Hyderabad for one week and our marriage was solemnised with the usual fanfare. Soon we left for Melbourne." Sangita narrated her story with tears in her eyes.

Sanjay consoled her: "Whatever you did is an image of the modern younger generation – a glimpse of the unprecedented influence of digital technology in their life. If we leave the sleep time, how long do we spend without a smartphone? Perhaps, not even half-hour! Internet and Google have become our new teacher, new adviser, new guide, and in many ways our life's manager. Now they have started gaining control over our emotions and thinking process, which is often conceived as the unification of man and machine."

"Your words have given me moral strength and new outlook. Until now, I considered myself an offender, a destroyer of established social values. I was consumed by the flow of time, I had lost the rein of wisdom. However, I learnt a costly lesson for the future."

"What happened after that?" asked Sanjay inquisitively.

"This is enough for today. Our first friendly meeting should not be burdened with sorrows."

They came out of the restaurant, exchanged their phone numbers, and said, "Good night."

The next week she faced two events which shattered her peace of mind. One morning, she was taking tea when there was a knock at her door. She saw two women standing, grim-faced, as if something serious had happened in the neighbourhood. "What's the matter," she asked politely.

"We are members of the local 'Women's Welfare Committee' - a voluntary organisation – which surveys the problems faced by women and tries to resolve them through mutual consultation; this also helps the government formulate socially useful policies. Since your divorce has occurred within three years of marriage, we would like to know why it happened – it was most unfortunate. You are not under any pressure, you can take part in this survey voluntarily and the information provided would remain confidential.

"In the Indian cultural tradition, the bond of marriage is considered long-lasting and sacred, and praised by the Western society. Then, why this tragic divorce? There must have been some extraordinary reasons."

Sangita was dumbfounded, perplexed, and in a dilemma. She said, "I need time to think over the matter, which is purely a private and personal issue. I would not like to reopen the painful pages of my past years and lose mental peace again. Yet, realising my social responsibility I might say something but at my own convenience. When I am ready, I will let you know."

"It's okay, as you deem fit. We sympathise with you."

Just after two days, Sangita read a brief report about her ex-husband in a prominent newspaper. As the report was accompanied with his photograph, there was no ambiguity about the identity. He was jailed for three months for being involved in a sex-related crime, and was he held in Perth. Though she was not in contact with him since long, she felt sorry for him - after all he was her first love, and she had enjoyed the thrills of romance in his arms. She realised he was a part of her life's history, like a part of her body, that could not be obliterated; her anger melted from inside, she did not take dinner that night.

She remained perturbed for several days, she did not know what to do. She wanted to call Sanjay, but lost courage; if she divulged this secret, she would have to recount the entire history – she hated this scenario. In midst of this stressful situation, she impulsively decided to see her ex-husband, Mohan. She moved on an unchartered path leaving the result on destiny!

The very next day, she reached Perth jail and waited for Mohan. He was startled to her – as if he saw a dreadful dream. "Don't be afraid, I am Sangita. I am angered at your criminal stupidity, but also deeply hurt. The path you had chosen has brought its curse on you. An invisible bond has brought me here - the shadow of history engulfed me when I learnt about your condition. But past and present do not co-exist, so are we. Human life is the priceless gift of God, live it righteously."

Mohan watched her like a statue, motionless and self-absorbed. Dejectedly, he said, "Presently, I am reaping the results of my wrong deeds; I feel honoured and comforted on seeing you here. I have heard that the 'bond of marriage' survives for 'seven lives' – I will wait for you in my next life." He was overwhelmed with emotions, he started sobbing, and his eyes were filled with tears; they sent a silent message.

"I had worshipped goddess Lakshmi during Diwali festival, and I have brought *prasad* (a part of sweets offered) for you. It symbolises the 'victory of justice over injustice' – so be it. I hope it helps you seek a new beginning in life." Sangita said wiping tears dripping from her eyes.

Her mobile phone started ringing, Sanjay was on the line. "Can we meet today?"

"I am in Perth. I will call you when I return."

Deliberately, Sangita did not call Sanjay for three-four days. She knew he would inquire about her divorce, and it won't be easy to side-track the subject. But how long could she hide the truth? Perhaps, it won't be prudent to do so either.

Within the next few days, they came for dinner in the same restaurant.

He started the conversation by asking, "Why did you go to Perth?"

She replied confidently: "Before that I will have to tell you about my divorce for which I am prepared today. Last time I was in a dilemma, but not now."

Her eyes were downcast, she was somewhat embarrassed, but she continued: "Soon after the wedding, I came to Melbourne with my husband. For the next two-three months there was excitement and youthful warmth in our sexual encounters, then, suddenly, I felt an unexpected withdrawal and laxity on his part. I imagined he had some mental anxiety, but he methodically completed other tasks including home keeping. Surprisingly, our sexual relationship decayed progressively in the following months; and I learnt that that he was bi-sexual and more inclined towards homosexuality. When I questioned him about his sexual orientation, he told defiantly: 'You can establish sexual relationship with anyone as per your choice, you have my permission.' It was like a bombshell – he encouraged me for prostitution! Since then I hated him, and our sexual relationship ended; I could not celebrate even our first wedding anniversary. In due course, we agreed to seek divorce with mutual consent."

Sanjay listened to her story attentively, and said, "These are the people who become sexual predators and entrap innocent girls in their nefarious networks. I am deeply pained at the distressful situation you faced, but I am relieved that you came out of this web in a sound shape. I greatly value your courage and resilience."

Then he asked, "Why did you go to Perth?"

She recounted, almost literally, what happened in Perth. She also told him about her discourse with the Women's Welfare Committee. "The heavy burden on my mind, sitting since long, has become much lighter. Now I can start searching for a new direction in life."

"I am proud of you! Even in very difficult circumstances you protected your cultural values – a feat to be admired. Giving Mohan the *prasad* of Lakshmi puja was a symbol of your extraordinary wisdom, which I sincerely respect." He added, "Consider me a friendly associate in your search for a new direction in life, I will not disappoint you. This is an occasion for introspection, and for celebration too. In its memory, champagne from my side – any objection?"

"As you like," Sangita surrendered, hesitatingly. She did not want to be discourteous.

Continuing the conversation, Sanjay said, "In this country different forms of sexual relationships have received social and legal sanction, traditional marriage between a man and a woman is no longer the only form, same sex marriage has been legalised, and the prevalence of live-in relationship between consenting partners is on the rise. Its long-term consequences on the social fabric are not known; only time will tell us, not pedantic debates."

"It is a very personal issue, no opinion should be thrust on anyone," said Sangita forcefully. The dinner time was over, they left the restaurant, and said "Good night."

Two weeks passed soon like a flying bird, while Sangita deliberated about her life's future. In her wisdom, the two most important points to consider were: (a) did she need a life partner? and (b) could she use her musical talents gainfully? She decided to consult Sanjay. Soon she received a call from him as if telepathy had worked! "My wife has returned from India. You are welcome at dinner, please note down my home address and try to come early."

"Does she know about me? Any cause of suspicion? I don't want to come between two of you; sometimes suspicion becomes an unmanageable mental disease," said Sangita, alarmed.

"Don't worry. I have briefed her about you, and her sympathy lies with you."

She spoke in a terse voice: "Hearing the word 'sympathy' time and again makes me feel as if I am a helpless creature, and this hurts my pride. You are my friend, and I expect to be treated like that – even when I take your advice or assistance." A bit of anger appeared on her face.

"I do apologise, that was never my intention. I praise your straightforward manners."

The sun was yet to go down below the horizon, but its rays had weakened. Sanjay and his wife were watering flowers in their garden when Sangita arrived. He received her courteously and introduced the two ladies: "This is my wife Rita, and this is my friend Sangita." Rita and Sangita greeted each other enthusiastically.

"Perhaps I came too early and encroached upon your private time - one hardly gets time to spend amidst beautiful flowers on a pleasant day. This suburb is more than twenty kilometres away from my place and I was coming to this side for the first time. Hence I started early to avoid being late."

"It is good that you came early, we will have more time for chit-chats. In this country all material comforts are available, but the pain of loneliness spoils happiness. Unoccupied mind wanders here and there – often towards unproductive thoughts." Rita's few words were enough to indicate her attitude towards living in a foreign society.

"Please come in," Rita invited Sangita, holding her hand lovingly.

Sangita was in a pensive mood; she vaguely thought that she had seen Rita in the past, but where? In Melbourne or Hyderabad? There was no possibility of a third place. Was it an illusion? Or an aberration? Her mind wandered, mentally she was away, while she sipped tea. "Are you unwell or tired?" asked Rita, finding her unusually quiet. "Nothing like that, I was enjoying your tea. Which brand is it?" "Have some more, it is soothing," replied Rita and went to bring another serve. Suddenly, a flash of memory hit Sangita: about a year ago, she had seen a woman coming out of a temple in Hyderabad and her face resembled Rita's. Was she really Rita? Or someone else? She had seen that face momentarily in a crowd and hence her recollection was hazy. She maintained outward composure, but her mind was racing.

Soon they assembled for the dinner. Rita was beautiful, and she appeared happy. *Then, why does she go away from Sanjay?* Sangita questioned herself. With a natural smile, Rita told Sangita, "I have cooked non-vegetarian Hyderabadi *pulav* (rice dish) especially for you. If it lacks in taste, don't feel shy to tell me – that's the way one learns." While she was serving food, Sangita saw three expensive, stone studded, rings on her fingers in one hand, and one engagement ring of solitaire diamond in the other hand. She self-analysed: *Wearing one engagement ring is quite common, but what could be the purpose of wearing three heavy rings loaded with different kinds of precious stones? This is hardly recommended by local beauticians.*

"*Pulav* is very tasty, where did you learn to cook this dish?" Sangita praised her.

"In Hyderabad, during my recent visit. My mother cooks very tasty dishes," replied Rita, pleased.

Jokingly, but meaningfully, Sangita commented, "Does one need shining rings for that? You have very expensive rings on your fingers, do they help you in any way?" "You played a joke on me unwittingly," Rita said, "but I don't mind." Hesitatingly, she added, "There is a story behind those rings." Sangita tried to know about the story, but Rita changed the subject, saying: "You sing very well, can we have a flavour of that? Singing is a great art." Sanjay dittoed her proposal.

After dinner, they were seated in the living room. "What kind of song do you prefer?"

"Any kind of lyrical song will do. These days, most of the Bollywood songs are devoid of rhythms, they are video inspired – not for listening intently with closed eyes." Sangita agreed with this observation and she sang two love songs. Then she recited one *bhajan* - devotional song – which enchanted everyone.

Sanjay concluded, "One hardly finds such a combination of godly devotion and sublime love interwoven in words. This form of creative presentation works like an interface between two generations – old and new – and you should keep it alive."

A question flashed in her mind: Can I use my musical training for a professional career?

Almost three months passed. Rita and Sangita talked on phone several times but they did not get a chance to meet. This time, Rita said, "On the eve of the forthcoming new year, Sanjay has planned to hold a party at our home and you are invited. Also, if you could come to my house within the next two-three days, we can finalise the menu – food is always a big item in any party. I would appreciate your help and company." Sangita thought she might get a chance to learn about the '*story of rings*' and she happily agreed.

It was lunchtime when Sangita arrived. Rita was alone, she received her affectionately. "Food is ready, it has to be warmed up. In the meantime, get soft drink from the fridge. If you like, we can have wine as well – Sanjay has stored a good collection."

"Red or white?" asked Sangita, while Rita was in the kitchen.

"As per your choice. Read the label on the bottle – some brands have a higher concentration of alcohol. I have no restriction, but I don't know about you." "Today, even a stronger brand will do. If I get intoxicated, you can manage," said Sangita jokingly.

"Why not? Sanjay has gone for an official tour for a couple of days – it's a day of women's freedom!" replied Rita teasingly. They laughed open heartedly, forgetting all the stress.

Sangita realised that Rita was a lively person, witty and cordial, and of modern attitudes. She could become a good friend – a rare commodity in an alien society. Rita thought similarly, she also needed a companion.

They spent a carefree day, chatting and singing, which was partly influenced by alcohol; and decided the dinner menu for about one dozen guests and allocated the responsibilities. Sangita will prepare tandoori chicken and *Gulab jamun*, Rita will cook other veg and non-veg dishes, and Sanjay will buy sweets and drinks from the supermarket. Sipping coffee, Sangita inquired: "Would you like to share the story of your rings? I guess it would be interesting – I am also curious to know." "I will tell you at the opportune time." This much indication was enough for Sangita, perhaps the story was full of mystery.

Sangita continued the conversation: "You might be feeling bored at home without much work to do, while Sanjay has a busy work-schedule. In such situations one gets depressed, which is a bane of this mechanical society. You should remain busy – you may enrol for some studies or take training in fine arts, etc. Then you can spend your time meaningfully and become a part of the social mainstream. Just try, you will find this society is also attractive."

"What you say is right; I also think so." Rita's answered briefly.

Sangita looked at her watch, it was time to go. Rita told her, "I have packed some food in a box for your dinner. One thing more – the party will continue till late in the night, come prepared for the night-stay. And don't forget to bring your diary of songs."

"As you wish. Today, I have found a sister." Sangita became emotional.

The much-awaited day arrived. Sangita reached early so that she could help Rita. Guests were expected to arrive any moment, when Rita gave Sangita a packet saying, "Put on this dress, most probably you will like it."

"What's this? I don't believe in giving gifts and that's why I didn't bring any."

"This is not a gift as a matter of formality. On the other day, you called me a sister and I greatly value this honour. Hence, I have bought a dress for you, which matches with mine," said Rita.

Touched by these words, Sangita simply uttered, "I don't know whether I would be able to repay this debt of affection." She hugged Rita, tears of joy appeared in her eyes.

It was a pleasant evening, quite congenial for a lively party. Rita introduced Sangita to all the guests, "This is Sangita, my sister-like friend, and known to Sanjay from his college days. And, true to her name, she sings in a melodious voice." Sangita was profusely greeted by all.

The party started with drink and finger-food, and the inevitable table gossips. The deliciously cooked tandoori chicken became a favourite item; some of the women invited Sangita in advance for the next party. By the time dinner was served, she had become acquainted with the guests; she also enjoyed their company. Later, she fully entertained them with her melodious singing; on her urging Rita and other women also participated in singing – some for the first time! One of Sanjay's friends said there was a great demand for Bollywood songs and dance, and he advised Sangita to start a *Sangeet Vidyalaya* - music school – in this area. This proposal was enthusiastically supported by all including Rita and Sanjay; and Sangita saw a new ray of hope. "The proposal is laudable, but it needs financial and physical support. It would be difficult to shoulder the responsibility all alone," she observed. Thoughtfully, Sanjay said, "You can get a loan from the local Bank, for which I can become a guarantor. And Rita would like to become your associate, she has good management skills."

The hall resounded with clapping. "This is a new year gift for Sangita and Rita!" At that very moment, colourful firework covered the television screen with the message 'Happy New Year'. Rita opened the cork of a champagne bottle – it was free for all.

Two years passed. The music school started running and it was recognised by the local government. Sangita's musical talents flourished, and Rita devoted a lot of time in overseeing the school's activities. In a way, it was a new life for both – they seemed happy and satisfied. Sanjay also felt pleased at their association and, more importantly, seeing Rita's positive attitude in day-to-day life.

One day, Rita told Sanjay, "I would like to go to Hyderabad and see my mother. It is more than two years since I met her; last night I saw a bad dream about her. I have talked to her on phone, she seems a bit unwell but there is no cause of anxiety."

"Yes, why not? Sangita can manage the school; I can help her when needed." He was rather delighted that she was going after more than two years. "If required, I can join you there at a short notice – don't worry. Your mother is a pious lady, she can fight any evil force with godly blessings."

The very next day, she told Sangita about her plan and added, "I will try to return soon. In fact, I also feel attached to the school which is a symbol of our efforts and confidence, and I don't want to loosen this bond."

Once in Hyderabad, Rita went to the office her astrologer whom she had already consulted more than once in the past. Reading her horoscope and palm-lines, the learned astrologer said, "The ill effects of the unfavourable stars on your life are coming to an end; you will be blessed with a child in near future. But, for that, you will have to wear a ring of *Navaratna* (nine jewels) henceforth."

"Has the effect of those three rings ended?" Rita asked anxiously.

"Certainly not. In effect, they have sheltered you from the wicked gaze of those unfavourable stars - and they are still doing that. You must continue wearing them as well. Have faith, your wishes will be fulfilled." The astrologer announced in a grave tone looking straight into her eyes. Frightened at his gesture, she hurriedly left his office; she had read in newspapers how some of the so-called religious gurus hypnotised women and sexually exploited them.

After she regained her confidence, she went to a temple, offered prayers, and asked blessings for having a child. There she met two of her college friends who had already become mothers, and this intensified her desire for having a child. She heard a voice: *Motherhood is the best ornament of a woman!*

After she returned to Melbourne, she seemed self-absorbed; her agility was missing, and she behaved erratically. As a way of starting the conversation, Sangita observed, "Your fourth ring is exceedingly beautiful - it looks heavy and very expensive. Don't you feel pain in your fingers?" Obviously, her old curiosity about the expensive rings was hidden in this innocent expression.

"Your eyes are always on my rings; next time I will bring one for you," replied Rita, feeling a bit irritated. She covered the rings with her sari and avoided Sangita's gaze.

"I am sorry, if you felt inconvenienced." Sangita supressed her curiosity and kept quiet.

One year passed. Rita faithfully followed the instructions of the astrologer, but she did not find any symptom of being pregnant. She felt devastated, her belief in the astrologer's predictions evaporated; and she threw away all the rings. "What's the matter? Where are your rings?" asked Sanjay at the dinner time. Rita started sobbing, tears fell from her eyes, and she told him the entire story. "I had that suspicion, but I left the decision on you. Now we will face it together," he said fondly.

The very next day, they were before their doctor who ordered some tests and advised them to avoid unnecessary worries and mental tension. "What will I tell Sangita? She will definitely ask why I removed all the rings from my fingers," Rita was worried. "Tell her that your fingers are having pain, and that's why you have removed the rings," suggested Sanjay.

On the way back, she continued talking: "The culture I come from believes in gods and goddesses, and people have faith in pundits and astrologers; even the educated class - including political leaders, Bollywood stars, wealthy businessmen – is not immune to this. The age-old practice of matching the horoscopes of the would-be brides and grooms continues despite modern outlook, and it is those astrologers who often decide the auspicious hour for solemnising the bond of marriage. In recent years, Prime Ministers have taken the oath of office at the hour appointed by their astrologers! Some fellows have declared themselves 'god' and they have large followers. Seeing these practices, I got attracted towards an astrologer – that was not unnatural."

Sanjay argued: "The difference between 'intelligent belief' and 'blind faith' comes to light at a late stage, often after the damage has been done. Science does not give credence to any belief until it is proven time and again through objective experiments. Is there any astrologer whose predictions have materialised again and again? Or whose rings or blessings have borne fruit all the time? The results of these practices are random, not based on any logic. There are some patients who take medicines prescribed by doctors, but on being cured they give credit to blessings bestowed by religious gurus or astrologers. This is the paradox of belief!" Then he realised his own fault: *Did he ever try to understand the desire of his wife? After all, they were living together since last five years.*

After a few days, they were again present in the doctor's clinic. The doctor told Sanjay, "Whatever I am going to say could have a long-term effect on your life, but such situations are not extraordinary. As per initial tests, you are capable of being a father, but your wife lacks the ability to become a mother. Even then, I am sending her to a medical consultant for a second opinion; the full report would be available within the next two-three months." Hearing this heart-shattering news, Rita started crying; Sanjay pacified her with consolatory words, and added, "No one has seen the cycle of fate – on such occasions one senses its invisible presence." He was equally dejected.

Time was passing fast. Rita's natural agility was eclipsed, she seemed to pass time with a vacant mind. When Sangita saw her visiting the doctor's clinic more frequently, she asked, "Is there something serious? Can I help in any manner? I am aware of my responsibility as your younger sister – give me a chance." "You will know everything at the right moment, have patience for the time being," replied Rita cordially.

Sanjay was mindful of the doctor's advice "try to avoid mental tension". Their wedding anniversary was approaching; at his persuasion Rita agreed to spend a few days at the seacoast. While preparing for the same, they received a phone call from the doctor "I would like to see you both tomorrow at ten o'clock". Their heartbeat increased; Rita was gripped with an unknown fear; they could hardly sleep in the night. The doctor told her, "You cannot become a mother, but the number of women like you is increasing day by day. It is not your fault - it's dictated by the nature. If you believe in God, consider it His merciful act or the cruelty of destiny. Accepting its consequences, try to dream for a happy future." Rita was dumbfounded, she covered her face.

"Then, what is your suggestion?" asked Sanjay desperately. "With mutual consent, you can adopt an infant. The second option involves 'surrogacy', if a healthy woman agrees to become the 'surrogate mother' of your child. But taking any hasty decision in this regard is not advisable, both of you must be mentally prepared. In this journey, you may consider me your well-wisher." Rita listened to what the doctor said, digesting its implications.

She remained glued to herself, deeply engrossed: *Did she spoil the valuable years in running after astrologers and in propitiating gods and goddesses? If so, she won't be able to condone herself.* She told Sanjay, "Drop the idea of going to seacoast, my heart is sinking with grief."

"Why so? The doctor advised us to consider our future course of action calmly, free from mental tension. Spending a few days in a camp at the seacoast would be refreshing; we can examine the pros and cons of any decision with an open mind. He also told it was none of your fault - it's a biological defect beyond anybody's control. Then, why to repent over it?" Sanjay embraced her, she felt the warmth and surrendered in his arms; such moments serve as a soothing medicine – a boon of the conjugal life.

The seacoast was throbbing with life, different from the cycle of daily routine. They saw families walking and swimming with their small kids; together they made sand castles, pyramids, and played footy. Spontaneously, Rita quipped, *"Children are like beautiful flowers; womanhood is incomplete without motherhood!"* Sanjay was sitting close to her, he was moved. Taking a deep breath, he added, "I agree with what you have said. I also feel that life becomes a lonely desert without children, and the weight of this situation grows heavier as years pass."

"I want to take Sangita into confidence, there is always a question in her eyes. Maintaining secrecy any longer may create a cleavage in our relationship, and she may feel alienated. She calls me sister, and I don't want to lose that respect." Rita said thoughtfully.

"You are absolutely right. Tell her your story, this will unburden your mind. Perhaps, she can help you arrive at the right decision as well."

Soon she invited Sangita for lunch. "Today, I will tell you my story." "I was waiting for it since long," replied Sangita. Sipping coffee, Rita described, very patiently, most of the events which had touched her life from early years till today; that included the astrologer's musings and the *story of rings*. Sangita was puzzled, rather perturbed; she did not know how to respond at this critical juncture. She managed to say, "How could you endure this mental agony for years? Was I not worthy of sharing your grief?" She was overwhelmed by emotional waves arising in her heart.

"You have already suffered excruciatingly painful episodes in your life – all by yourself. I always admire your forbearance, courage, and compassionate manners; and this has taught me a useful lesson. You are a source of strength to me in many ways," Rita said overcoming her own sadness.

"Your perception that *'womanhood is incomplete without motherhood'* is highly emotional and psychologically corrosive; you will have to come out of this state of mind. Life moves ahead on the earthly realities, not on sentiments; I have myself experimented with them." Both sympathy and inspiration were hidden in Sangita's words.

"Perhaps, you are right. Then, what should we do? We have two options."

"We will think over it. And we need time for that." She looked at the clock and left.

Sangita went to bed early, she was also perturbed. Rita's words *'womanhood is incomplete without motherhood'* were haunting her, though she had kept her weakness under control. The depth of these words, and their worldly reality, made her restless – after all she was also a woman. The forgotten chapter of her life came to life: *by now, she would have celebrated the seventh anniversary of her wedding, and she could have become a lucky mother.* Several questions erupted in her mind: *Did she make a mistake in fulfilling the role gifted to a woman? Did she ignore her cultural traditions in the turbulent flow of modernity? Could she become a mother if she married again?* She fell asleep pondering over these matters.

On the other side, Sanjay and Rita were also struggling with the doctor's advice. He asked, "What have you decided about the doctor's advice?"

Rita said, "I was thinking over the matter for the last few days. I am not in favor of adopting an unknown infant, because he will possess absolutely no part of us – you or me; I mean that not even a thread of our genes will be ingrained in him. I will always feel guilty of stealing someone else's precious wealth, as if I have grabbed the jewel of a helpless woman. Moreover, no one knows whether he will accept us as his parents or search for his biological parents when he grows up. His hereditary traits can also become a reason for distrust and separation."

"Then, we are left with the second option only. Sometimes I feel why to bother about having a child at all. There are many great men and women in this world who are childless, and who are happily devoted to public service. We can do the same."

"You are talking about a third option, and I don't approve it," uttered Rita indignantly. "As you like," Sanjay surrendered, though half-heartedly.

Rita made up her mind: Sanjay was healthy, his hair was still black, he was medically fit to father a child, and he would cooperate in having a child through surrogacy. What she needed was a healthy and respectful woman who could realise their sentiments and agree to become the 'surrogate mother' of Sanjay's baby. It was a complicated question, but its solution was not impossible. Surrogacy had become socially acceptable and legally allowed – of course not everywhere. When she told Sanjay about her resolve, he agreed in principle. The next step was to give it a practical shape.

At the dinner table, Rita told him: "According to newspapers the practice of surrogacy has flourished rapidly in Thailand and India, especially among poor women for the sake of monetary benefits. Reliable sources indicate that some non-profit agencies and unscrupulous doctors are also involved in underhand dealings for their own benefits, and hence surrogacy is emerging as a pseudo trade. It is difficult to say what the truth is, but it is well-known that many wealthy Australians have utilized their services. It is always prudent to use the services of qualified doctors and we are financially capable of that. We do not want to take undue advantage of the difficult social and economic condition of a woman, rather we wish that she leads a respectable life free from any stigma."

"The human angle in your observation is praiseworthy and I fully endorse it. You may apprise your mother of these developments and urge her to search for a suitable woman in Hyderabad itself. If she succeeds, that would be very helpful."

"Your suggestion is quite logical, but it might be full of hurdles. My parents are old-fashioned, nurtured in traditional values, and religious minded. They will consider 'surrogacy' against their religious convictions and disdainful. I would not like to hurt their feelings," said Sangita cautiously.

Sanjay added, "I would also like to alert you to some of the predicaments which often disturb me. A few weeks ago, there was a chilling news on the television: 'A surrogate mother gave birth to two babies, one of them was mentally retarded who was disowned by the Australian father. This has become an issue of human rights, very complicated and unresolved.' Another example is even more interesting: 'A surrogate mother refused to hand over the infant to the biological father; she spontaneously developed strong motherly love and the whole society sympathized with her. Nobody cared about the mental agony and the financial loss caused to the biological father.' There could be many such cases that we are not aware of. No one can predict what traumatic situation arises and when; we will cross the bridge when we come to it."

"Whatever you have said are exceptions, which rarely occur. You must have heard the dictum: *exceptions justify the rule!* We should be optimist – this is the way the world moves ahead. If we don't play mischief with anyone, if our intentions are honest, God will help us." Rita's pious nature came to the fore, her eyes were beaming self-confidence.

"My dilemma is over, I am with you." Sanjay asserted.

After consulting some of the health professionals Sanjay learnt about a clinic in Delhi where surrogacy was undertaken, but he was required to go there to complete the legal formalities. At the same time, finding a capable woman was of primary importance – though an arduous and complicated task. "Could Sangita be of any assistance?" he asked Rita. "A good idea!"

Rita decided to take Sangita into her confidence; she invited her for the afternoon tea.

"What's the matter? Sadness has covered your face," Sangita said, "as if a deep anxiety has made home in your mind."

"The story is long, we will talk leisurely," replied Rita, with an artificial smile.

When Rita placed a kettle on the stove for making tea, Sangita held her hand, saying "let me do it and you take rest". "That's why I see the image of my younger sister in you," complemented Rita. Both felt the sensation of an unseen bond that joined their perceptions.

Sipping tea, Rita described in detail what had happened after they received the doctor's advice; that included their decision of having a child through surrogacy. Sangita became sentimental: "Under compelling circumstances, I was deprived of motherhood. I would have forgotten my eternal pain by holding your cute child in my lap. I never imagined the destiny would be so harsh." Their combined sadness made the atmosphere burdensome, rather dreadful. Warm tears rolled down their cheeks; there was no one else to share their agony or to console them at this juncture.

Regaining her senses, Rita enquired, "Do you consider my decision right? Besides Sanjay and me, no one knows about it - not even our parents."

"The decision you have taken is based on logic and faith, which seems appropriate today. But no one has seen the future. If your resolution is firm, all hurdles can be overcome; and the outcome will be enjoyable. If you need my assistance at any stage, don't feel shy to tell me. You call me younger sister, give this relationship a chance to mature." Sangita's words were soothing and meaningful.

Encouraged by these words, Rita added: "Now I feel more assured. Our first step is to search for a compatible woman who willingly agrees to become the surrogate mother of Sanjay's child; and she will also have to satisfy certain requisites. Sanjay is in mid-thirty, healthy, well educated, and he comes from a family of high social status. The woman who becomes the mother of his child should come from a similar level as far as possible, otherwise our parents will feel uncomfortable. What could be the future of a child who fails to get the love and affection of elders? Though we have been living in this country for several years, we cannot disregard the traditions of our family in India. The thinking of the second or third generation could be different, but that won't be our concern."

"It appears you are still carrying the burden of the caste system and the mind-set of its social hierarchy. Your marriage was arranged by your parents, it is they who found Sanjay for you; they decided the merits of the would-be groom – perhaps your choice did not matter. It is surprising that you want to swim in the same cultural flow while living in a modern global society." Sangita seemed frustrated, her voice showed a degree of bitterness.

Rita protested, "I am not beholden to caste system. It is dying even in India; then how can it survive here? In my opinion, social status refers to education, profession, family background, etc. It is important to know whether a woman undertakes surrogacy as a profitable business or as an altruistic service to the needy couple deprived of one of the most enjoyable blessings of life."

Sangita relented, and asked, "Do you want to examine her? If yes, then how?"

"Not the kind of examination you have in mind. I just want to ask a few simple questions: How far have you studied? Are you married? How many kids do you have? How do you manage your household expenses? Have you worked as a surrogate mother in the past? What is your religious faith? Any woman is not a machine for giving birth to children – whether a traditional mother or a surrogate mother. She must have emotional inspiration for giving birth to a child, and an attachment towards the baby in her womb. These unseen forces influence the natural development of the baby."

While they were engaged in the discourse, the doorbell rang. Rita opened the door; Sanjay was standing with bags in his hands. "I can make tea," offered Sangita and went into the kitchen.

"What were you talking about in my absence? Can I know or is it confidential between the two of you?" said Sanjay humorously. Rita recounted the entire conversation; wherever she missed the link, Sangita reminded her.

Taking a deep breath, Sanjay said, "It appears that both of you are agreeable on this matter. But I would like to make one thing clear: I will not talk to any woman for becoming a surrogate mother, especially for my child. In fact, I won't be able to face that woman. I am ready to handle the legal aspects and to meet the expenses." Rita and Sangita saw each other with the same question in their eyes: what will happen now? They didn't know how to respond to this situation.

"Let's come into the kitchen, it's almost dinner time," Rita waved to Sangita.

"Sister, what will happen now? Can you fulfil this task alone? I am getting fearful."

"You are staying here tonight. We will think over this matter in the morning with fresh minds."

Rita was mentally distressed, she could hardly sleep that night. Sangita's condition was not much different. Early in the morning, they assembled for tea while Sanjay was still in the bed. Rita said, "I kept on pondering for the whole night, then I saw a ray of hope. I would like to take you to Delhi, this will give me the much-needed companionship and the moral strength. Most probably our task will not be completed in a single visit, but we will get some experience. Surrogacy is a new subject for both of us." Surprised at the proposal, she replied impulsively, "Let it be so, if that is what you want. I will try to remain with you like your shadow, but I will not ask any question or intervene in your work. I am still fearful – see my heart is pounding."

Rita was seated before the Chief Administrator of a surrogacy clinic in Delhi, and Sangita was standing behind her. He read the letter of the Melbourne doctor, and after preliminary inquiry lead her to the office of the senior physician.

After examining all the medical reports of the couple, Sanjay and Rita, the physician told her: "I have a list of about one hundred women who have agreed to undertake surrogacy and their brief introduction is also available. Some of them had taken part in surrogacy in earlier years – quite successfully - and some of them are new. I intend to choose three or four women from this list who could be the 'surrogate mother' of your husband's child. The final decision will be taken after consulting both the parties – the chosen woman and Sanjay – and after satisfying the legal requirements."

"Can I ask them some questions? The introduction you have compiled would be helpful; but talking to those women could be more revealing – after all surrogacy is a very personal experience." Rita said, fixing her eyes on the physician's face.

"You can meet those women, talk to them, but one trained employee of the clinic will always be present. This is to ensure that no misunderstanding is created, and no offensive questions are asked. In the case of foreign clients, one needs extra caution.

For example, language could become a barrier or ethical issues might obscure the basic objective, etc." The physician was considerate - he sympathized with Rita and protected the interest of the clinic as well.

Not fully satisfied with the physician's offer, Rita argued: "As a conscientious woman, I strongly believe in protecting the honour and dignity of women; I don't intend to hurt their pride. But it is equally important to peep into the background of the woman who is likely to be the *surrogate mother* of my husband's child. Quite possibly she may not talk freely in the presence of a clinic's staff, which is not unusual, and therefore I would like to talk to her when none else is present. If she does not want to answer any of my questions, she can do that. She will be under no undue pressure to reveal any private information either. This process will be praiseworthy for your clinic, and it will also enhance your personal reputation."

After a few moments of thoughtful silence, the physician responded, "I trust you and admire your vision. I am inclined to give you the required permission as a matter of exception, which is often denied by the administration. However, there are some conditions: you will not talk to any woman for more than fifteen minutes; you will not talk about money matters; you will not record the conversation; and this arrangement will remain confidential."

"I accept these conditions; and thanks for your kind gesture." Happiness appeared on Rita's face, as if she had won a battle.

After two days of anxious wait, she was permitted to see three women. She talked to them one by one in one of the clinic's rooms and asked a few questions as she had already decided; she took extra care to look polite and sincere. She always opened the conversation saying: 'I am unfortunate, and I seek God's blessings through you', which showed how obliged she was to see them. This created a sense of affinity and encouraged them to talk freely on the concerned issues. Sangita remained outside the room but she could see all the women closely and study their body language when they emerged from the room.

As soon as Rita emerged from the room, Sangita asked excitedly, "Did they answer your questions truthfully? Did anyone pass the exam?"

"How was your assessment? You saw them closely. As a student of psychology, you might have read about one's facial expression."

"Their body language was lacking enthusiasm, but my guess could be wrong."

"We will talk about it later. Let's go to the hotel." She closed the discourse sharply.

Rita remained silent for the whole journey; Sangita also kept quiet. This was an indication of a turmoil in Rita's mind, she needed rest and solitude. On the pretext of making a long-distance phone call, Sangita stayed in the hotel lobby while Rita proceeded to the room. When Sangita returned after an hour, Rita uttered herself, "Whatever the women said from their perspective was not unexpected. I was surprised that each one of them enquired how much money they would be paid and requested me not to tell this to any official of the clinic. As per one of the agreed conditions, I was not allowed to discuss money matters and hence I ignored this question. Soon sadness covered their face and they became suspicious of my intentions. I felt self-defeated, nonplussed."

"Mutual trust is essential in the matter of 'surrogacy'. You can meet those three women privately through an employee of the clinic, and that can be arranged by spending some extra money. After all, money has its own power!" suggested Sangita.

"Do you mean by bribing them?" Rita said in a terse voice.

"I don't care whether you call it bribe or inducement or reward; but it provides a pathway."

"How can you guarantee that this information will not reach the physicians? If they learn about it, they will never trust us in future – rather they will hate us for committing an act of treachery. And those women may be harmed, which will be intolerable for all of us."

"Your suspicion is plausible, but what's the way out? Just leave and go back?" Sangita was annoyed that her suggestion was brushed aside so casually.

In a pacifying tone, Rita explained her point of view: "In my opinion these women are facing financial hardship, the painful burden of poverty, and hence they want to earn a handsome amount of money through surrogacy. At the same time, they are apprehensive whether the clinic will compensate them adequately. If that is the case, it amounts to exploitation of the hapless women and an unethical trade, which is reprehensible. Those women must be knowing that rich foreign clients spend a fortune on surrogate mothers, and that's why they asked me how much money they would get. I can't be a party to this short of harassment to helpless women."

"Your guess is absolutely right, but how can we fight the system? The clinic might be having powerful links or political patronage as well," responded Sangita, dejectedly.

"We need time to think over the matter; we will return to Australia tomorrow. I will inform the physician before that."

More than three weeks had passed since they returned to Melbourne, but the symptoms of mental tension were still visible on Rita's face. She seemed irritated, and absent-minded. Sanjay again became concerned about her mental state and he talked to Sangita about it. Empathetically, she said, "I can understand your distress, it's taking your toll as well. The deep-rooted anxiety in the sister's mind is eating away her self-confidence. She is looking for 'surrogacy' on her terms, but the ground realities are much different. This conflict is going on in her mind, which also perturbs me now and then."

Sanjay was convinced that Rita needed psychological support more than anything else. At the dinner table, he impressed on her the importance of living a self-contended life. "It is hardly desirable to sacrifice the peace of mind for the sake of having a child; there are many couples in our category. Also, it is not the time to be pessimistic, we can explore other channels. In such matters, patience brings fruition. Anxiety erodes wisdom!"

"You are right; pessimism is not the solution of any problem."

Just then she got a phone call from Sangita: "The students have proposed to hold a short entertainment program at the music school in the coming week, which will also be an occasion to showcase their talents to the community. If it succeeds, we can organize a music conference on a bigger scale. Sister, you have remained mostly aloof from the school's activities for the past two-three months, but this is no longer acceptable - we need your active participation. Together we can create a good future for the school."

"It is a very good proposal. Tomorrow, we will discuss the details in the school."

"One thing more: talk to Sanjay also. Maybe, we need some assistance from outside."

When Sanjay heard about it, he felt pleased and thanked Sangita for her astute planning. "It might be the beginning of a new chapter!" he exclaimed.

That day finally arrived. The students' parents and community members - many of whom had helped in the establishment of the music school – were seated as planned. The names of the students who were to sing songs, recite poems and tell satires at the podium were prepared in advance. It was agreed that Rita would be the master of ceremonies, while Sangita would work in the green-room and dress the participants in fanciful attires. After a long time, Rita gave life to her ornaments; they were smiling with brilliance in bright light. Commencing the program, she said, "The art of singing is like a divine gift, it relates to human feelings and works as a cultural ambassador. It transcends the boundaries of race, religion, language, and geographical separation; songs are powerful agents of cross-cultural integration and they generate a sense of togetherness among different communities. The popularity of Bollywood films is a credible testimony to that effect - people from different backgrounds and cultures enjoy Hindi songs and often dance to their tunes." The audience applauded her through prolonged clapping.

One by one, the students enchanted the audience through their performance. Their colourful dresses, intricately designed, presented a small exhibition of the Indian arts! Finally, a ten-year-old child recited a poem which touched the emotional chord of many people.

"In the ocean of feelings, I search for that pearl
which hides the mystery of my life's creation;
My heartbeats are pledged to that fatherly person
who gave the seed of life, traits, colour, and appearance;
A product of science experiment, I am called fatherless
who can't touch the dirty apron of the 'surrogate mother';
I dedicate my tears on you, craving for the parental bond
wherever is your destination – accept my hearty salutation."

A wave of affection ran among the audience. Obviously, the child was the product of 'surrogacy' and he was eager to see his biological parents; and he felt restless on such occasions. A deeply perturbed woman climbed on the podium and tightly hugged the child and started sobbing. Tears dropped from the eyes of many women; Rita and Sangita were also among them.

Before concluding the function, Rita requested John Wilson, the local Councilor, to say a few words on behalf of the invited guests. He said, "This program was entertaining as well as socially relevant. I admire all the students and organisers for their efforts. I would like to add that 'surrogacy' meets the demands of the modern society and I am not its opponent. But children born out of surrogacy have the right to know their biological parents and other related facts, without which their life may be stressed, and their progress may be adversely affected. Also, giving emotional support to such children in schools would be appreciated." Rita was so engrossed in her thoughts that she forgot to thank Mr. Wilson when he finished his talk.

Immediately, Sangita took the microphone in her hand and said, "We have just seen the spontaneous display of motherly affection by many of you – it will not go in vain. We would remain alert to children's feelings, and their latent aspirations; perhaps that will give them new inspiration. All of you ...."

Before Sangita could finish the sentence, someone from the audience interrupted saying: "I have heard that you are an accomplished singer with a melodious voice. The power of songs is universal, it alleviates internal bitterness and cools the agitated mind. This is very much needed at present." Many from the audience, including some women, urged her to share her musical talent. She had to agree: "Please give me ten minutes to get ready. In the meantime, you can have tea/coffee."

When Sangita played on her *Veena* (musical instrument), she seemed totally occupied in a meditative mood and the audience felt enchanted, rather hypnotized. She sang the famous bhajan: *"Maiya moree main naheen maakhan khaayo, Gwaal baal sab bair karat hain barabas mukh lapataayon, Maiyaa moree main naheen maakhan khaayo, ..."* This passage of the celebrated Indian poet, Soordas, brings to life the essence of motherly love for a small child. It was well suited to the occasion and people gave her a standing ovation.

The program ended successfully. When people were leaving, a young man told Sangita, "When so much affection is embedded in your song, one can only imagine how much lies in your real life! *Your kids must be fortunate – don't allow this motherly bond to dry."* Sangita was puzzled at his comments, she wanted to respond but restrained herself; perhaps he was unaware of her situation. She moved ahead, but his words echoed in her mind.

On returning home Rita went straight to her bed room and closed the door from inside. She wanted privacy and silence, where she could hear her heartbeats only; she was facing mental upheaval. She had taken a copy of the child's poem which she read several times, and each time she got a new message. She felt as if her own feelings had taken a lively form – she also wished that a child born through surrogacy knew his/her biological parents. She felt vindicated and resolved to tread on this path with greater confidence.

On the other hand, Sangita was tired, she seemed perplexed but did not know why; she missed her dinner and went to bed early. She tried reading a women's magazine but could not concentrate. Then she phoned Rita, but it was Sanjay who replied, "Rita is resting in her room. Is there anything important? There is weakness in your voice, why so? Today's program was wonderful, you should be happy." "Thanks for your help in organizing the event; I will talk to her tomorrow." She ended the conversation sooner than expected.

After initial uneasiness, she went into deep slumber. She heard in the dream: '*Your kids must be fortunate – don't allow this motherly bond to dry.*' Startled, she woke up. She ignored it, considered it a random thought without much significance. Soon, another voice echoed in her ears: '*Womanhood is incomplete without motherhood.*' She became fearful – was it a game of destiny? After much effort she slept, but she heard the same voice again; her fear compounded. The night's end was coming soon; the dawn was knocking at the horizon. She had heard from elders 'dreams of early morning are meaningful' – then what could be its consequence? She self-reasoned: *Who was that young man? Why did he say so? Was he attracted towards her? Had I known his phone number, I might have called him. But he knew me as a teacher at the music school, and he might contact me. I should remain alert!*

Early in the morning, she received a call from Rita: "Did you call me last night? What's the matter? Anything important?"

"My mind is wandering; an unknown fear has gripped me. I want to see you."

"The school is closed today, come at lunchtime."

Rita embraced Sangita when she alighted from the car. "I was waiting for you, why were you late?"

"There was heavy traffic on the road, and my thoughts were roaming like uncontrolled clouds. Hence, I drove a bit slowly."

"Okay. Now you can feel assured. We will have tea first and then lunch. – I presume you are not too hungry. This will give us ample of time for chatting; Sanjay will not be here until early evening." Rita went into the kitchen to prepare tea.

"The truth is that my hunger has ended after last night's dream; and an unknown fear has gripped my mind," said Sangita in a trembling tone.

"You call me elder sister, isn't it? You can freely share your worries with me, that will reduce your mental stress and we can find a solution as well," suggested Rita affectionately.

Sangita described what she saw in the dream and wondered what that meant. She added, "I don't believe in dreams, and they have no scientific basis either. Despite that, it has made me fearful for the first time. I had seen many good and bad dreams related to my life over the years, but I hardly cared for anyone. Why has it terribly affected me this time?"

Rita was about to drink her tea, but her fingers seemed immobilized out of nervousness! She placed the cup on the table and looked at Sangita with sharp eyes. "What's the matter, sister? Are you all right? Why are you quivering?" asked Sangita, feeling concerned.

"I suddenly felt dizziness in my head. Now I am all right."

Sangita was intelligent and the struggles she faced had made her more judicious and foresighted. She anticipated that Rita was also gripped with some mysteries which were related to her own dreams, but she did not pursue the matter. It was also possible that Rita knew that young man, but no conclusion could be drawn.

They finished their tea quietly, no one tried to break the silence. By that time, Rita had become normal and she invited

Sangita into the kitchen for preparing lunch. Eating a piece of fried potato, Sangita said, "Sister, you have not said anything about my dreams. Are they always meaningless? Or simply mental illusions? Do they have some purpose? If not, why an unwanted burden on the mind when sleeping? Is it not a wastage of biological energy? Dreams arise from mental activity – neurons' stimulation - which consumes energy."

Rita listened attentively and then replied, "You have asked a volley of questions which have no proven answers. You were a student of psychology and hence you are in a better position to analyze them. I simply believe that no natural process is purposeless; all physical and mental activities are integral to life's sustenance; but our understanding is limited. Dreams are also like other biological functions; they are a product of the intelligent human machine; they developed at certain stage in the evolutionary process. We are not capable of deciphering their meaning and purpose." She explained her position on the vexed question of dreams. Explaining her position on the vexed question of dreams, she admitted that she was not professionally qualified to assert her views.

"Sister, you have almost given an interesting lecture on dreams. The purpose of dreams is a mystery, and their explanation has no definite methodology. However, it believed that dreams are a means of fulfilling those desires which have remained unfulfilled in real life. In other words, our hidden ambitions become explicit and satisfied in the world of dreams, but even this perception is controversial – not accepted universally. Dreams are peculiar in their forms and contents, and often strange; it is difficult to understand their actual purpose."

"Then it may not be totally out of place if I say that your dreams manifest your 'desire for motherhood' and inspire you to fulfill it. Sometime ago, you had said that your earnest desire for becoming a mother could not be fruitful because of adverse circumstances; in other words, your intense desire remained unfulfilled. It is up to you to accept or reject this notion, but you must think over it with a cool mind." Sangita was stunned; what Rita said had a grain of truth.

Two weeks passed. Rita continued going to school and she kept an eye on Sangita's activities. After a discourse on dream-related matters, Sangita had become a bit reserved, perhaps she was struggling with some internal dilemma. Rita had wanted to reopen this issue and apologize to her if she was hurt in any manner, but she could not get the right opportunity - sometimes good intentions lose their impact in the absence of a congenial atmosphere. One day, she saw Sangita talking to someone on phone for a long time in a jovial mood. Soon thereafter, she told Rita, "Sister, my friend is coming to Australia on holidays and she would like to visit a few iconic places of interest. She is from Hyderabad, the same city we come from. If you can accompany us, that would be wonderful and most enjoyable; it will also remove your boredom. I would suggest her to come here during the forthcoming school holidays so that students do not miss classes." "The proposal seems interesting, but I cannot make any commitment without asking Sanjay," replied Rita enthusiastically.

The next day Rita called Sangita, "For touring major cities and seeing the widely spread natural bounties of Australia, one should have a powerful car at one's disposal or hire it locally. I don't like driving long distances and I can't negotiate the clumsy roads of a metropolis. Also, you will need at least eight to ten days just for visiting the few major places of tourists' attraction. I don't know how capable you are to undertake this journey on your own."

"Your assessment is absolutely right; and my physical capacity is also limited. Then, what to do? My friend is likely to come here very soon."

"If you suggest, I can ask Sanjay – he may agree to come along."

"I have no objection. In fact, he will be a great help."

"What about your friend? Is she engaged? Or recently married?"

"She knows nothing about Sanjay; why should she have any reservation? And why the second question?"

"I asked casually, though sometimes it becomes relevant."

"It appears you want to keep Sanjay bound by a pillar," said Sangita jokingly.

"Haven't you heard – a horse runs after green grass!" Rita said with a big laugh.

Their distraction disappeared, and they felt lighthearted again. A bout of cordiality quenched the heat of unintended conflict, if it ever existed.

The following week, Sangita received her friend at the airport; Rita also accompanied her with a bouquet of fresh flowers. She introduced them, "This is my intimate friend Rita, and this is Helen Jackson – my college friend."

Giving flowers, Rita said, "You are most welcome. Melbourne weather is tricky, but most enjoyable during this time of the year."

"Sangita had told me that you are like her elder sister; I would be honoured to get a similar treatment," said Helen with due respect.

"You are right, I also appreciate this sisterly bond," Rita replied with a smile.

She concluded that Helen was educated, civilized, and skillful in conversation; apart from being beautiful, smart, and attractive. Guessing her curiosity, Sangita added, "Helen is a nurse in a government hospital and she is completing a course in information technology through a distance education provider."

They spent some time in small gossips and soon reached Sangita's home. Before leaving, Rita invited Sangita and Helen for dinner. They were to leave on the trip just after one day for which Sanjay had already made the necessary arrangements.

They were ready to start for the journey when Rita said, "Helen, you may occupy the front seat by the driver's side; Sanjay will tell you about the important historical monuments that come on the way. He has done that for me in the past; he is very knowledgeable."

"No, that place is for the wife or the girlfriend. I will take the back seat along with Sangita."

"If we can simply remain friends for a few days, no formality will be needed," said Sanjay.

Sangita intervened, "I fully agree. I am seeing for the first time that you are also jolly-minded, until now you always behaved like a serious person." Rita supported her, and the whole atmosphere became friendlier. The days flew fast like a bird. During those carefree days they played games, sang songs, relaxed on seashores, learnt surfing, dived under water, snapped pictures, visited museums, and enjoyed a variety of international foods including the very Australian 'Fish and Chips'. It appeared as if they became younger by five years! Helen was mesmerized at the sight of the Great Barrier Reef and its natural grandeur; and she spent hours at Harbour Bridge, Opera House, Taronga Zoo – all in Sydney – and mingled with tourists on the Gold Coast in Queensland. While returning, Sanjay drove on the Great Ocean Road - the spectacular coastal road in Victoria and a must for the nature lovers.

It was the last day of the trip. As the weather was hot, Sanjay parked his car under a tree, and all of them came out for a short rest. While seated on the lawn, Rita said, "It is a good occasion that we say something about this 'friendship trip' and that is recorded. It will be a valuable gift for all of us, especially for Helen who can carry it in her smartphone." "Why not? A very good proposal," agreed others in one voice. The question arose: who will be the first? Sangita suggested 'decide it by a lottery'. Accordingly, Sanjay was the first in the lot. He said:

Sangita is wise and polite, and dear to us
and her melodious songs warm our hearts,
She is a source of joyful light
and she brings with her a flowery delight.
In Helen's smiles lies an erotic sensation
without which life is devoid of exhilaration,

Time goes fast in her company
day and night lose their obvious meaning.
But Rita's affection is beyond description
she is the real queen of my life's garden!

Rita was pleasantly surprised, she impulsively kissed Sanjay, and uttered, "Despite living together for the past several years, I could not relish your poetic love. Today I feel blessed to hear your sweet words; their emotional appeal has touched my senses." Then she thanked Sangita and Helen whose goodwill could make it possible.

Sangita was mesmerized, she felt immersed in the ocean of Sanjay's goodwill and affinity. Overwhelmed, she quipped, "I was aware of the sister's boundless love, but I have realized Sanjay's tender feelings during this trip only. It is like a new light of hope, that will always remain with me – unblemished, unquenched." Tears of joys appeared in her eyes.

Helen, in her turn, added, "I have enjoyed the happiness of years within a few days! Rita and Sanjay are two priceless jewels, never to be lost. Sangita is fortunate to be associated with them, so am I." She kissed Rita's hands affectionately.

It was time to move. Rita felt a mild pain in her stomach, she needed rest. She took a pain-relieving tablet and sat comfortably on the car's back seat, and Sangita came on the front seat. Soon the car was cruising on the freeway.

Sangita was facing a mental turmoil, a volley of questions had erupted in her mind: *What is meant by 'flowery delight?' And by 'source of joyful light?' These words indicate intimacy, closeness. Did Sanjay say so just casually or deliberately? If intentionally, what did he think? Does he love me? Do I also like him?* She closed her eyes and got lost in a dreamland! Very soon, the rein of wisdom played its role: *How could she think so even for a moment? It amounted to committing a crime. After all Sanjay is her sister's precious possession! It is unethical to nurture a feeling of intimate love towards him.* Once more the wisdom surrendered before the sentiment, and she started debating with herself: *I can control myself, but what if Sanjay insisted? It is difficult to stop love's tide – she had experienced it in the past – what will she do now? It was the first occasion to assess him from a close distance, he can be an ideal partner. Had he not been married, I would have sacrificed myself at the altar of his love! People say everything is fair in love and war! Is it right?*

She looked towards Sanjay obliquely, she wanted to read his facial expression. She recalled the well-known couplet of the great Hindi poet Raheem: *"khair, khoon, khansee, khushee, bair, preeti, madhupaan; Raheeman daabe na dabe jaanat sakal jahaan."* Accordingly, a jubilant feeling of love leaves its impression on the face! She wondered: was it on his face? Suddenly, he commented, "You seem too serious, what's the matter? Are you anxious about something?"

She was startled, did not know what to say. Hastily, she managed to utter, "I don't know whether the *joyful light* you have seen is a sheer imagination or has an element of reality."

Sanjay replied cryptically, "You must have heard the idiom: *chiraag tale andhera*, that is, darkness under the lamp."

"What does it mean? I don't understand your mysterious language."

"Okay, let me explain: for receiving a lamp's light, one has to stay a bit away from it. It has a second meaning, that you can deduce yourself."

Sangita kept quiet, thinking: *Is Rita at the centre of the second meaning? Inscrutable!*

Helen had left for Hyderabad a few days ago. Sangita's daily routine had also become normal except that she felt loneliness. Today was a public holiday, so she remained in her bed lazily till late in the morning. In fact, the same thoughts, which she nurtured in Sanjay's company, gripped her again last night and therefore she was somewhat absent-minded. She was planning to visit Rita, when she received her call, "I would like to see you today; it's a public holiday, we can chat leisurely."

"What's the matter, sister? If it is urgent, I can come within a short time."

"No, you won't have to rush. I want to come to you and ask for something. You must have heard the proverb: *the thirsty man goes to the well; the well doesn't go to the thirsty man.*" Rita said hastily.

Sangita replies with modesty, "You have equal rights on whatever I possess, then why to ask? I call you sister, it is not without meaning."

"I intend to come in the afternoon, is it all right?" asked Rita cutting short the conversation.

"Okay, around four o'clock. I will wait for you," confirmed Sangita, a bit alarmed.

Suspicions arose in Sangita's mind: *"Did Sanjay say something? Did his laudatory words about me create a misunderstanding? Or is it related to our cryptic conversation in the car? Maybe, Rita could see my hidden attraction towards Sanjay – after all she is an intelligent woman!"* Her heartbeat increased, she trembled with an unknown fear.

When Rita reached Sangita's apartment, she was warmly welcomed. "Your hands are very cold, why so? Any sickness?" asked Rita, showing sisterly anxiety.

"How can I explain, sister? My hands are getting cold out of nervousness. I don't know what you will demand and whether I would be able to fulfill," replied Sangita, feeling shaky as if she was appearing at an exam.

"Nothing like that, mad girl! I will never misuse your trust or make any harsh demand that you cannot fulfill. The decision will be yours, have faith in God."

"I am getting restless - tell me at once whatever it is; I can't brook further delay," uttered Sangita with excitement in a loud voice.

"Then, listen carefully. You should become the surrogate mother of Sanjay's child. This is my demand, and my earnest desire." Rita said with a cool mind, looking reserved and confident.

Hearing this, Sangita jumped as if bitten by a scorpion! She felt as if someone had exploded a bomb on her head, and she fell on the sofa – almost losing her senses! Rita gave her support, patted her back, and said in a motherly tone, "I am not your enemy. Don't lose patience, have faith in me."

Sangita regained her composure after a while and controlled herself. Then she said, "Sister, tell me once more what you have said. Maybe, my ears deceived me, and I became emotionally disturbed." Rita repeated verbatim what she had said, and added, "I sincerely wish that you become the surrogate mother of Sanjay's child, you are most suited for that."

Sangita started crying like a child, streams of warm tears rolled down her cheeks. "Sister, what short of sacrifice you are exacting from me? What kind of examination is it?" She uttered in a panicky voice.

"It is neither an examination nor a sacrifice. Think sensibly, take recourse to your wisdom, and ask your heart. I don't want your answer at this moment, take your time. In fact, such decisions are not taken in a haste, they need the consent of heart and mind both. Before taking a final decision, give me a chance to explain my perspective as well," pleaded Rita who was also overwhelmed. She wiped Sangita's tears with her apron and then her own. Both needed some time to control their emotional tides; they were facing the tempest of their lives.

Breaking the long silence, Sangita responded, "Perhaps, you are right." She was depressed, but not delirious.

"Come on, let us prepare tea. I am getting hungry," said Rita purposefully searching for lighter moments and a fresh opening.

Taking a bite of *samosa*, Rita said, "My proposal respects the honour of womanhood and the prevalence of wisdom, the essential ingredients of our relationship. You are aware of my principles which are sacrosanct in choosing a woman who can become the surrogate mother of Sanjay's child; and on that touchstone you are the most suited person. You are healthy, beautiful, of the similar age, and not greedy for money.

Surrogacy is not a profitable trade for you, it is a voluntary act for society's welfare; and it would be a praiseworthy gift to our lives – including yours. Yes, it is important that you are found medically fit for it. This is what wisdom tells me." Then she added, "In my imagination, you have tender feelings for Sanjay and he is also friendly to you. These signs are also encouraging."

"And the honour of womanhood? How do you perceive it?" asked Sangita meekly.

Rita stated: "Both of us are women, and implicitly we treasure the importance of womanhood in our hearts. You might be remembering what I had said earlier: *womanhood is incomplete without motherhood,* that is, a woman's life remains unfulfilled without giving birth to a child. You had also said that *you remained deprived of motherhood because of cruel circumstances, and bad luck.* My conviction has not changed but I am medically unfit. However, you can change your fate – you can rejoice the pleasure of being a mother. Remember, one gets the real pleasure of motherhood only through the exciting experience of breastfeeding her baby, it has no substitute; this is my considered view."

She added, "Perhaps, you may choose another path to realise this dream; you can remarry and give birth to your husband's child. If you are ready for this, I would be happy to withdraw my proposal. And it is advisable to take such a decision without undue delay because childbirth in later years has its own complications – you can find them on the internet."

"What will I say to the society? How will I face their rhetorical satires?"

"You have already seen the ugly face of social reactions. In times of calamity, one depends upon one's own moral and spiritual strength, the wider society often remains a silent spectator. *It is your life, you will decide how to live it.* This is well accepted in this country, and this notion is also gaining ground in India. Besides this, I can assure you of my full support in any social struggle – I know my sisterly obligations."

"Sister, I have heard your views very attentively. But I need time to arrive at any conclusion."

"I had already told that such life-changing decisions are not taken in a haste; you can take your time. If you encounter any dilemma, tell me without hesitation. I am not only your 'sister' but a friend also. Whatever we have discussed will remain confined to us only; I will not divulge anything to Sanjay without your consent."

"Yes, that is the proper course," said Sangita taking a long breath.

"Your samosa was very tasty, Sanjay will also like it." Rita said, getting ready to go.

"Just wait, I will prepare a few for him."

For the next three-four days Sangita remained embroiled in her thoughts. The events of the last few months kept appearing before her eyes like lively images - day and night. For one moment she questioned Rita's intentions, her actual motives. She had read: *"Triya charitram, purushasya bhagyam, devo na jaanaati; kuto manushya."* That is, a woman's character and a man's fate cannot be deciphered even by gods; what to talk of humans! But she was forgetting that she was also a woman, and this dictum also applied to her! She was alerted by her wisdom: "There was no credible reason to doubt Rita's intentions, she had also advised you for remarriage. But, was it prudent to marry just for the sake of becoming a mother? Where was the guarantee that it would be fruitful? You are at the crossroads of life, choose a new direction." She decided to take a chance, perhaps it was fated! She phoned Rita, "Sister, I am ready for the medical test; you may fix up an appointment with the doctor."

One year later, Sangita gave birth to a son. His forehead was wide like Sanjay's and his curly hair resembled with Sangita's. She was overwhelmed, she was now a mother! She kissed him, touched his tender fingers, and brought him closer to her chest.

Rita's face beamed with happiness, when she said, "God has listened to our prayer, we bow before Him! This cute child will enlighten our lives; and he will have two mothers – Devaki and Yashoda! My sense of motherhood will also flourish in his company." Sanjay was standing at a distance, not sure what to say. Suddenly, he felt attracted and uttered, "Today, I bow before the wisdom of the two ladies! And a warm welcome to the little child."

Just then, a nurse came and asked, "What would be the name of this child?"

"Gopal Arora." Sangita said with confidence. "Is it all right, sister? Arora is Sanjay's surname, and Gopal is the second name of Krishna." Rita nodded her head in acceptance.

Almost two months passed like the twinkle of an eye! Sangita breastfed the child and cared for him - especially in the night losing her own sleep. During daytime Rita often took him to her home, but she had to call Sangita when he felt hungry – it was not easy for Rita to pacify a crying baby. Soon she told Sangita, "Try to keep him away from breastfeeding, now he can digest the formula milk. I would like that, after a month, he stays with me and you come here to assist me. I have already read several books on how to bring up a newly born child, and it has given me some confidence."

"*This child is your jewel, I am like a trustee.* How long can I keep him away from you?" Controlling over her emotions, she added, "I will do as you want, but my motherly love for him will always remain alive. After all, he is a part of my body, and my blood runs into his veins."

"There is one condition: you will never tell him that you are his biological mother. His mother's place is mine, and he will call you *mausi* (the mother's sister) as practiced in most of the Indian families."

"I fully understand it, you don't have to worry. If I could retain the respect of being your younger sister, that would be enough for me; it will sustain me like the proverbial nectar," said Sangita gracefully, winning over her sadness.

Time passed fast like a river's stream, silently and expediently. Gopal was now a ten-year-old boy, known for his sensible manners among his classmates. One day, he told Rita, "Whenever I am with the *mausi* I feel an unknown attraction towards her; her presence radiates a wave of intimate affection and goodwill. It appears as if she was my mother in the previous life, and that motherly bond casts its shadow on my present life. Mummy, do you believe in the past life? Does it affect our present?"

"Son, there is no credible evidence of the past life, but some people have faith in it. The Hindu religion does believe in the past life or rebirth, the so-called immortality of the soul. They also believe that the deeds, good or bad, of the previous life influence our life-journey in the present; that is, good deeds bring pleasurable blessings whereas evil deeds invite painful curse. Such descriptions are found in many of the mythological stories."

She added, "Sangita is your *mausi* as well as my intimate friend. We share our feelings, our emotions, our stories, and meet quite often which you must have seen. I presume the waves of my feelings also emanate from her heart and they reach you unhindered. You are very fortunate; she will give you what I can't – no one is perfect."

The birthday of Gopal arrived after a few weeks. As he was entering the second decade of his life, this event was celebrated with a big fanfare. Early in the morning, Sangita had gone to a nearby temple to seek blessings for Gopal and she purchased a gift for him. After all the guests had gone, she gave him a colourful packet.

"Mausi, what's in this packet?" asked Gopal with curiosity.
"Open and see."

He saw a small statue of Lord Krishna – as a child. Excitedly, he quipped, "This statue is very beautiful. I have read that he had two mothers – one who gave birth and the other one who brought him up. It must have been a divine blessing!" Sangita embraced him with moist eyes.

About a week later. Sanjay phoned Sangita in the middle of the night in a frightened tone, "Rita has suddenly developed severe headache, I am taking her to the local hospital. Can you manage Gopal tonight? He is getting panicky, he needs someone to console him."

"Why not? What am I for? You can drop him at my house while on way to the hospital. What happened so suddenly? Just last week she was so jubilant."

The next morning, he informed Sangita, "Rita has been administered an injection and she is asleep. The cause of her headache will be ascertained only after necessary tests, which might take three-four days." Though he appeared cool-headed from outside, he felt tormented seeing Rita's sudden illness.

He remembered praising her as the 'queen of his life's garden' – its real meaning had become apparent today when he felt dejected like a withered flower!

When she learnt about Rita's condition, Sangita became deeply worried and she decided to offer especial puja in the temple. She also assured Sanjay that she would take full care of Gopal until things became normal and Rita returned from the hospital; and advised him to concentrate on other matters.

A few days later Sanjay was present in the doctor's chamber, perspiration had appeared on his forehead out of nervousness. The doctor told him, "Mr Arora, your wife has a malignant tumour in her brain - a dangerous cancerous growth. She needs to be operated at the earliest. As the tumour lies in the interior part of the brain, it is difficult to predict about the success of the surgery and its ramifications. We will try our best. I can simply assure you that our expertise in this field matches the world's best. I hope your good luck prevails."

Darkness appeared before Sanjay's eyes, as if his world has been eclipsed. Taking control over himself, he said, "Doctor, please do what is best for the patient. The boat of my life is in your hands, only you can save it from sinking."

A day before the date of her surgery, Rita wrote a note, put it in a sealed envelope, and gave it to the head nurse, saying: "I know that my surgery is complicated. If I die or lose my memory, please give this envelope to my son Gopal. Kindly keep it safely." She felt defeated, she wondered if today's night could be her last! Gathering her courage, she decided to take dinner with Sanjay, Gopal, and Sangita. On her repeated requests, the doctor permitted her for going to the hospital's canteen and asked a nurse to keep an eye on her condition from a close distance.

She was elated, she informed Sanjay about tonight's dinner. "Should I bring something that you like? A sweet dish?" asked Sanjay. "No, nothing of that short. But bring that small idol of Lord Krishna, which was gifted to Gopal by Sangita. This way, I can sense their presence around me."

At the dinner table, Rita started serving dinner. Immediately, Sangita tried to take the rice bowl from her hand saying: "Sister, you are weak. Let me serve the dinner." Sanjay also said so.

"No, today I will serve the dinner. The merciful doctor has given me this chance, don't stop me. Who knows if I get another chance or not!"

Hearing this, Gopal hugged her tightly saying, "Mummy, why do you say so? You will come home very soon; don't lose your spirits. One needs willpower to fight a disease, it's like a powerful medicine." And he became emotionally choked, almost speechless.

Sanjay and Sangita were equally perturbed, mentally shocked. They could hardly say, "We should have faith in God."

"I also think so." A ray of joy flashed on Rita's face, when she urged, "Let us have dinner in a joyful mood, why to worry for tomorrow at the cost of today?"

Sangita withdrew into herself, she was suddenly stricken by a thought: *Chirag bujhane se pahale tej ho jaata hai,* that is, a lamp becomes brighter before extinguishing! She started sobbing, covered her face, and felt dejected. Sanjay realised Sangita's pain, but he kept quiet.

Rita was taken into the operation theatre at the appointed hour; Sanjay waited at the door with tearful eyes – alone and depressed. The last words said by her only minutes before echoed in his ears: "Goodbye until I return!" After several hours, he learnt that Rita was in the Intensive Care Unit and no one could be allowed to meet her. She was unconscious but alive, perhaps with the help of the modern machines, and this situation continued for two-three days. During these worrisome days Sangita prayed for Rita's recovery and gave moral support to Gopal. What else could she do!

Finally, that ill-fated day arrived. The doctor told Sanjay, "Despite our tireless efforts, we could not save Rita's life. The cancer had spread in her brain, like a silent thief."

Sanjay started sobbing holding Rita's lifeless body; Gopal grieved saying "Mummy, Mummy, ..." for long without any response – he saw a dead person for the first time. Sangita's condition was equally pitiable, she had lost a pillar of her life. The physical body made of *Panch-Tattva* was waiting to merge into the same. *(Panch-Tattva or Panch-Bhoota*: five elements of which human body is made of; they are: air, water, fire, earth, and space; a vision of the Hindu religion)

Shortly thereafter, the head nurse came and handed over an envelope to Gopal. "What's inside," he asked, bewildered.

"A day before the surgery, your mother gave this sealed envelope and told me to personally handover it to you in case she died or lost her memory. I don't know what's inside."

Gopal opened the envelope with trembling fingers. He found a brief note which said: "Sangita is your real mother, she gave birth to you. Give her full honour henceforth – this is my last wish. I apologise for hiding this fact from you until now." Soon he clung to Sangita who was standing beside; and she embraced him affectionately.

The cycle of time never stops, nor does it care for anyone. Time is also the most powerful bandage that heals the deepest wounds. Sanjay had thought that Gopal would adjust with time and gradually return to his normal activities; he had done the same remorsefully. He was mindful that Gopal was not inconvenienced in any perceptible way; and Sangita had also become more alert in discharging her responsibility as a mother. It appeared that everybody's life was coming on the normal track; time had healed their wounds to a great extent.

One day, Sanjay suddenly arrived at Sangita's home – unannounced, without intimation. She wondered: *what calamity has fallen this time!* Her face turned yellow out of unknown fear.

Looking at her frightened face, he said, "Don't be afraid; I have not come to demand anything; I just want to share my helplessness – possibly you can find a way out."

"Tell me, what's the matter? I do sympathise with you; have faith in me."

"Gopal has started going to school regularly and taking interest in his routine works. These good signs ...."

Sangita interrupted midway before he could finish the sentence, and said tersely, "Then, what anxiety? What short of compulsion?"

Sanjay described the situation in an afflicted tone: "It is more than two months since Rita expired, but even now Gopal gets up in the night blurting "mummy, mummy"; and on several occasions he ran into my bedroom looking for Rita. I thought he is a child, and his mental attachment towards Rita would decline as time passes. I didn't tell you about these things, I didn't want to unnecessarily harass you – after all you have your own life. But last night he asked me two questions which I could not answer, and possibly these questions are tormenting him. I was alarmed at his mental state and I felt compelled to seek your advice."

"You can confide in me, tell me everything without inhibition."

Last night we were taking dinner. During that time Gopal asked, "Do I have the permission to address Sangita *mausi* as mummy? The late mother's last wishes won't be fulfilled without it." Lines of anxiety appeared over Sanjay's forehead, he wondered if Sangita could solve this riddle.

"And the second question?" asked Sangita, showing signs of restlessness.

"The second question was more complicated, rather disturbing. That's why I came running to you forgetting that I didn't even inform you. His queried, 'If Sangita *mausi* is my real mother, then why does she live alone and separately? Is it not against the values of the Indian culture?'"

Sangita was stunned! Dumbfounded! She could not believe that Gopal had become so matured! She didn't know what to say at the spur of the moment. Breaking the overbearing silence, Sanjay said, "In my opinion, Gopal should be made aware of the mystery of his birth, but I can't do that. There exists an unseen sacred bond between a mother and her child - just like divine consciousness. You will have to find a way out, I am simply clueless."

"I don't see an easy way either. Gopal is sentimental, and our sole duty is to ensure his progress without unwanted mental burden." Then she added, "Wait for a while, I am going to prepare tea for you. This will also give you some time to think over the matter calmly; maybe, a ray of light flashes in your mind."

Sipping tea, he uttered hesitatingly, "A thought has emerged in my mind. But I need your permission to divulge it. And forgive me, if it hurts your pride."

"Why this formality? Tell me with an open mind." "I have two vacant rooms in my house, you can live in one of them." Sanjay said, looking into her eyes intently.

Puzzled, Sangita felt suffocated at his words. She gasped for breath! She was frozen like a statue – *kaato to khoon naheen*! (A Hindi proverb meaning sudden impact that leaves one speechless, etc) She was quiet, debating in her mind. There was pin-drop silence in the room, which was interrupted by the tick ... tick ... sound of the wall clock. Soon, the clock also became restless, it seemed to 'tick' more frequently! After five minutes, Sanjay's heartbeat became faster, he became fearful, and asked in a raised voice, "Are you all right, Sangita?"

She came alive from a deep slumber, and uttered, "I was in the dreamland: to meet the sister's self and to get her blessing! How can I reside in a house where her larger-than-life shadow pervades?"

Then she said thoughtfully, in a serious tone, "There is one condition: I was your friend, I am your friend, and I will remain your friend. Nothing beyond that."

"Yes, I agree."

4. Message of Midnight

"Who?"

No reply. Soon the same knock at the door – khut, khut, khut! It was late in the night, and deep silence prevailed all around. Vinayak was alone at home, his eyes were fixed on a computer screen. By profession, he was a journalist and he was writing a report on domestic violence. He had just written 'Conflict within family is spreading like a contagious disease, this is causing social disruption and it often takes the form of physical violence ...' when he heard the same sound. Annoyed, he asked again, "Who?" But the same silence, no reply. When he looked through a window, he panicked – a young woman in wet cloths was standing in a huddled state. It was drizzling outside.

Opening the door, he said in a low voice, "Please come in, you are almost wet. It appears you were out on the road since long."

"Thanks for your goodness," she said. She started sobbing.

"Bathroom is just behind you. Please change your dress, you will find some of my wife's attires in the closet. She has gone away for a week," said Vinayak courteously, "and you are in a safe place."

By the time she came out, Vinayak had already placed hot tea and biscuits at the central table.

Feeling obliged, and a bit uncomfortable, she spoke in a shaky voice, "There was no need for taking this trouble. I am hardly hungry, fear has quenched my hunger." Hesitatingly, she picked one biscuit and placed one in his plate; and picked up her cup of tea.

They remained silent while taking tea, her eyes were downcast. Ultimately, it was Vinayak who broke the silence: "I am Vinayak, a journalist, living here for the past three-four years. Would you tell me something about yourself? Please don't be shy and be assured that you are safe here."

"My name is Meena Chopra, I have adopted the surname of my husband. We got married only two years ago and we are living in an adjoining suburb."

"What's the reason for leaving home at this odd hour? You must have had a compelling reason for taking this step. Possibly, you had an unpleasant argument with your husband, but why did you take such a drastic decision? You could have at least waited for the next morning - didn't you think of any frightful occurrence?" Vinayak seemed impatient to know the background of her action.

"It is a long story and I don't want to entangle you in its details. We were having arguments for the past three-four days, even very confronting ones, but today the guy crossed all limits. Sandeep, my husband, was in rage, it seemed he would soon assault me. I was frightened, so I fled away without thinking of the consequences. By chance, I read the nameplate in front of your house: Vinayak and Sarita Sinha. These are Indian names, I saw a light of hope in the darkness, and I knocked at your door."

"This is a clear-cut case of domestic violence, you can call the police for protection. These days newspapers, television channels, and social media are full of reports on such events – it appears they are spreading like a communicable infection. The government and several social organisations are providing help to victims in various ways. You can call the police from here, if you so decide. I fully sympathise with you, and Sarita will not hesitate in supporting you as a sisterly woman – you can rely on her."

Taking a deep breath, she uttered, "Police can give a temporary protection, but they cannot find a permanent solution. And this will make our families bitter enemies, which is unacceptable."

"Which families are you talking about? Do they live in this city? Taking their help could be most desirable - you may call them, or I can call on your behalf." Vinayak seemed relieved thinking of a logical way out from the vexed problem.

"You are so innocent! Sandeep's and my parents live in India – in different cities but not far from each other. They had arranged our wedding with much fanfare. At that time, Sandeep was in Melbourne and I was a college student living with my parents. We two had met earlier, and we liked each other."

"Then why this sudden conflict? Why this dislike and fear of physical violence?" Vinayak was perplexed at the state of their relationship.

"Just leave these matters. I presume Sandeep was under the influence of alcohol, he will start looking for me after his rage gets watered down and I don't want that he comes here. It is summer time, only three-four hours are left before the dawn and I would like to get out before that. By that time, my cloths will become dry."

"Where can you go alone? You might be attacked. I can escort you to your home and talk to Sandeep as well."

"This is not needed at all. You gave me shelter when I was helpless, I am grateful for that. Please go to your bedroom, and I will also take rest on this sofa."

"Okay, let it be so. When the time is ripe, kindly knock at the door."

Meena fell flat on the sofa, closed her eyes, but could not sleep. She tossed up and down, her mind was engaged in self-debate – whether she could have saved the situation. The dawn arrived silently within hours; she put on her own clothes, and uttered meekly, "Vinayak ji, the night has ended. It is time to go now."

Rising from his bed half-asleep, Sandeep exclaimed, "Where will you go?"

"There is a park in the vicinity of my house, Sandeep will definitely come there searching for me. He has not lost all the traditional values - a fraction remains alive in his heart and mind. He loses his wisdom when excessively angry, but often recovers from this mental state." She explained calmly.

Vinayak suggested, "You go ahead, and I will follow you from a distance. In this way, I can keep an eye on you until the daylight breaks. No one in the park will suspect that we know each other."

"You are so kind-hearted! You care for my safety." Both walked towards the park.

Within an hour, he saw a young man moving fast towards Meena. It was Sandeep. He found his estranged wife and she accompanied him voluntarily. Vinayak returned satisfied.

After two weeks. Vinayak received an unstamped, and unaddressed, envelope in his mail box. He reasoned: *someone must have dropped it personally.* On a careful examination, he could see the word *Meena* written faintly in small letters in a corner of the white envelope. His heartbeat suddenly increased - by now he had almost forgotten the episode related to her. Placing that envelope in Sarita's hand, he said, "I am feeling a bit nervous, you should open it. I am afraid if something inauspicious has happened." He had already briefed Sarita about Meena and her situation, so she also became alarmed.

"On the coming Saturday, I will wait for you at 4 pm at the coffee shop located in the eastern corner of the shopping centre, possibly it will be our last meeting." Sarita read this message and handed the letter over to Vinayak. Keeping silence for some time in a pensive mood, he said, "It is difficult to derive any conclusion from this message: *Where is she going? Why is she going? Is she going alone or with Sandeep?*

Sarita protested: "You are simply using your brain, not the heart. This is usual for men, nothing especial about you. It is obvious that Meena is under acute mental stress, perhaps she is getting frustrated from her life. In this situation, she can take any unthinkable step; she needs sympathy and support from friends and well-wishers. She considers you a well-wisher – a drowning person will clutch at a straw! Try to meet her."

"But I have neither her phone number nor her home address."

"Then, wait until Saturday," she pronounced in a sorrowful tone. There is nothing we can do until then!

"You will have to accompany me, I can't face her alone. Even otherwise, a woman can feel the pain of another woman's heart more genuinely."

It was Saturday afternoon. The shopping centre was crowded, Vinayak and Sarita were among them. Well before the appointed time, they walked into the food court, purchased coffee, and occupied a corner table. His watch read quarter to four, he surveyed the stream of incoming people, but Meena was nowhere. He appeared tense, when Sarita said, "You should occupy another table because Meena might hesitate in approaching you in my presence."

"It seems appropriate," he replied and moved to another table.

It was almost four o'clock when he could see Meena entering the food court. She had already seen him from a distance and she waved to him. Her face was covered with a layer of sadness, her movement was burdensome. She joined the queue at the coffee shop. Coming forward, he told her, "Today, you are my guest. Let me buy coffee, you can occupy the table in the meantime. Yes, please tell me – how much sugar? One teaspoon or two?"

She said softly, "You have honoured me by coming here - what can be a better gift? This will double the coffee's sweetness - one teaspoon is enough!"

While sipping coffee, her eyes were downcast. A conflict was going in her mind and heart: *Is it proper to share her personal situation with Vinayak?* The shyness of womanhood was getting powerful over reasoning.

Breaking the monotonous silence, Vinayak said, "I am fearful of an unknown suspicion - what's the meaning of *last meeting*? Like a friend, you can tell me about your situation without hesitation; I am also curious to know how the matter has come to this point."

Suddenly, she exclaimed, "Alas, I wish your wife were here! I would have seen my sister's image in her, ..." And she started sobbing. Perplexed, Vinayak signalled Sarita to come and join them.

Putting her hand on Meena's head, Sarita said, "Please stop crying, I am here to share your agony. Vinayak has already told me about your situation, and I fully sympathise with you. I also understand the inherent shyness in a woman's character, in fact a woman's shyness is her ornament. You can share your story with me in confidence." Hearing this conversation, Vinayak volunteered: "I am going away for some time, both of you may continue. Call me, if needed."

Controlling her emotions, Meena said, "Sister, you are like my elder sister - mature and affectionate. Why to hide from you? Relationship between me and Sandeep has soured, and there is no time to explain the reasons. It appears he is likely to divorce me soon. I am not afraid of the divorce, but there is another aspect which is torturing me internally." Suddenly, she stopped talking.

"Why did you stop so suddenly? What's that aspect that is bothering you? When you give me the honour of being a sister, it bestows upon me some obligations as well. It is my duty to encourage you to share your feelings and intentions." Sarita's words were consolatory and powerful.

"I am pregnant, it was confirmed only last week, and Sandeep is not aware of it. Once he knows, he may exert unwanted pressure on me for an abortion. But I want to be the mother of my child – this is the unique gift of womanhood," said Meena reluctantly.

Sarita was dumbfounded, the problem was complex. She could not decide what to say or how to help the hapless lady. Taking a deep breath, she spoke, "Have you thought of a credible solution? I fully agree with your resolution, taking decisions in such matters is the right of every woman."

"I am leaving for my country next week; and I do not want that Sandeep knows about my condition. I have told him that I am going to see my sick mother, but I will not return before giving birth to my child."

"Then, what short of help do you expect from us?"

"It is quite possible that Sandeep will file a divorce petition. In that case I need time for submitting my reply – the case must not be decided without hearing me. Please keep my phone number and my home address."

"It is a normal procedure - the court will definitely give you a chance."

"In the Western countries, including Australia, allowing a divorce on flimsy grounds is not uncommon, and that is socially acceptable. There are cases where divorce and re-marriage occur more than once in someone's life, but that is against our culture. I am a citizen of India, protected by the Indian constitution, and hence I won't be bound by the decision of an Australian court.

"In this country, divorce is considered an economic issue – money in exchange for divorce. But in India, the social context is more important. A woman divorcee passes through social stigma, cultural shock, and humiliation; and often her entire life gets ruined. My situation is much more complicated, as a child is growing in my womb. If he does not survive because of my mental agony, who will be responsible for that murder? It is important to place these matters before the court of law."

Sarita was emotionally overwhelmed. "I will be a partner in your struggle. Today, I have realised the glory of cultural identity - keep it preserved."

Just at that moment, Vinayak joined them. "What were you talking about? Both of you seem exhausted. Another round of coffee?" he broke the ongoing conversation.

Sarita recounted the full details of their discourse while Meena kept quiet.

Thoughtfully, he quipped, "I am a journalist, my pen will work for you."

Three weeks had passed since Meena left. Vinayak suddenly saw Sandeep in a restaurant – he was having coffee and his eyes were fixed on a newspaper. Vinayak also bought a cup of coffee and came at the same table. They greeted each other casually. After a while, Vinayak said, "Your coffee is getting cold, but you are busy in reading. Is there something important?" Sandeep pushed the newspaper towards him, saying: "You can read it yourself."

The title of the article was "Clash of Cultures". An American youth had married an Indian girl three-four years ago - the girl was educated, smart, and they had met before their marriage. They were yet to celebrate their first wedding anniversary when friction cropped up in their day-to-day life. They tried to patch up and lessen their ideological differences, but that did not last long; their relationship became tense – leading towards harassment and psychological assault. When the wife learnt that she was pregnant, she fled stealthily to her parents in India; she was afraid that her husband might force her to abort. Soon thereafter the husband filed a divorce petition in America, where divorce is often allowed with suitable monetary compensation. But the wife responded by filing a counter petition in India and rejecting the idea of divorce, saying: "As a citizen of India, I am protected by the Indian constitution. Therefore, my case should be decided by the provisions of the Indian laws." It is well known that getting a divorce in India is a lengthy and complex process. She had also argued, "The court must consider the human aspect of the situation. If the child in my womb does not survive because of my mental agony, who will be responsible for his murder?" The legal arguments are going on and both sides are incurring heavy financial losses; it is only the attorneys who are benefitting.

The articled informed about another interesting case. An Australian resident applied for the immigration of his wives more than two months ago. He has two wives, but Australia gives legal recognition to only one wife. He is required to divorce one of them, otherwise he might lose both. This is a debatable complicated problem that defies a simple solution. Such intricate issues seem to emerge from cross-cultural clashes in a globalised society.

Returning the newspaper, Vinayak queried, "Are you also facing a similar conflicting situation?"

"Why did you think so?" Sandeep said and moved away, annoyed. In fact, he was mentally entangled in a similar web, but he did not want to divulge. Just two days ago, he had learnt that Meena was pregnant when he saw a booklet *Precautions during First Pregnancy* sent by her doctor.

Tonight, Sandeep could not sleep, he was restless. Whatever he read in the newspaper resembled the story of his own conjugal life – bitter and baneful. Perhaps, the fate has given him a warning! It was a chance that he had time to read the article or was it fated? The old scenes started emerging before his eyes: the beautifully sculpted body of Meena, her attraction, her agility, her skilfulness, and the initial few months of their intimate love. Then why this clash? Intolerance? Tension? Yes, he was financially stressed, but she was very cooperative and ready to share the burden. Whenever he was in an angry mood, she tried to mollify him. He realised that he had crossed the boundary of civilised behaviour, he felt remorse and self-humiliation. He reasoned: *The financial hardship would go away sooner or later, but what about the life's crisis? He will have to surmount this hurdle – but how? A broken glass can be glued, but the mark remains visible! Could he win Meena's trust again? How heartless he is that he has not phoned her even once?*

On the other hand, it was Vinayak who had written that article in the newspaper and he wanted to know Sandeep's reaction. He thought of a scheme - he had experience in investigative journalism. Within a few days, Sarita came to Sandeep's home and told him, "I am writing an essay on the domestic problems of women and I would like to meet your wife in this regard."

"I am alone."

"Are you unmarried? Or have you divorced your wife?"

"It is not necessary to answer such questions," replied Sandeep angrily.

"I will come again. Please remain ready to give the correct information, otherwise I will have to obtain it from the municipal office." Sarita said in an authoritative tone.

She had almost left, when he said, "Please come in, I would like to say something."

In a gentle voice, he narrated, "A sense of bitterness has cropped up in our relationship. My wife is pregnant, and a few weeks ago she left for her parents' home without telling me. Now I am remorseful and ashamed of my behaviour. If the child in her womb suffers from any harmful medical condition because of her distressful situation, I would not be able to condone myself. I am dumbfounded, I don't know what to do. If she returns, she will have my full sympathy and ..." Before he could finish the sentence, he broke down – tears dropped from his eyes.

"Woman's heart is tender, it has space for love and compassion both. She can be a wife, and a mother too. If you give her one ounce of love, she will return four times." Sarita spoke in a friendly tone.

"Then, what should I do? Please show me the right path." Sandeep spoke eagerly.

"Give me her phone number, I will talk to her. There is one condition – I can meet her whenever I want," she threw her last dice.

"I accept willingly." Sandeep seemed relieved, he found a well-wisher.

It was past midnight. Meena was half-awake when her phone rang.

"Who is calling?"

"I am Sarita. Listen to what I say, very carefully." Then she described in detail what had happened: the contents of the newspaper's articled written by Vinayak and the main points of her interview with Sandeep. "Life does not move on a straight line like a train, it faces ups and downs. It involves occasional confrontation as well as timely surrender - they do not diminish the intensity of the relationship. To pardon is woman's ornament, try it once for the sake of the child in your womb."

Meena became emotional, she started sobbing. Controlling over her feelings, she said, "Sister, I get moral strength from what you have said. What is your command for me?"

"I can't issue any command - it's your life – but I have a suggestion."

"I have called you sister; your advice will be a blessing for me," said Meena thoughtfully.

"I would like to welcome you at the airport."

"Sister, that day won't be far away! This *Midnight Message* is like a new source of light. I hope its spark will guide our path in the future."

"God bless you!"

5. Narrow Lane

Sandeep stopped his car. He was looking for the street named 'Narrow Lane' but the GPS, the global positioning system, was not able to locate. He had already entered the village, Rampur, but its roads were beyond the Google's digital eyes. He got down from the car and asked a villager for help.

"Who do you want to meet?" queried the villager in a rough tone.

"Why? Is it necessary to name the resident for locating a street?" replied Sandeep casually.

"Ok, then please tell me your name and address. This village is like a big family, it has not caught the manners of a town where people are often self-centred. Therefore, we try to know the whereabouts of a newcomer, especially in the present uncertain times and chaos."

"My name is Sandeep Sharma and I live in the district headquarters about 50 kilometres from here. You might have gone there – villagers come there for a variety of official works. Your name?"

"I am Sanjay Singh, the owner of a grocery shop just around here. I know most of the residents as they are my customers. Many of them buy on credit and occasionally I also borrow from them. This has kept the rural culture alive, but it may not survive much longer."

Before Sandeep could react, he continued: "You have come in a shining car, it must be yours, and it is obvious that you are from a rich family. Then, what relation do you have with this remote village? Are you a government officer? They do come here occasionally, mark their presence, and return without making their shoes dirty. Most probably, your car will get stuck in the mud and hordes of curious onlookers will annoy you as well."

Angered, Sandeep said, "You ask so many questions, as if I am a thief or suspicious alien. I am not a government officer either, and I don't intend to harass you. I might ask someone else." He almost reached his car when Sanjay spoke, "Please leave your car here, it will remain safe. Take left turn from here, and then take first right turn after a while. Within a few minutes you will see Hanuman Temple, take right turn there onto Narrow Lane. In case of any difficulty, just call me – here is my mobile phone number."

Sandeep was a young civil engineer. He had obtained the engineering degree four years ago and then a diploma in management. Presently, he was a partner in a consultancy firm and committed to his works. As development fever had gripped the state, the construction of roads, building, and other infrastructure was in full swing; it was in this context that he was here to survey the village. Rampur was well-known for its good school, and it caught the attention of politicians because of its large population that played a vital role in democracy. A proposal for all-round development of this village was recently approved by the government. Before he started for the trip, an officer of the company told him, "You must visit Narrow Lane." But he didn't explain the reason despite Sandeep's request. It appeared mysterious and made a mark in his mind.

Following Sanjay's instructions, Sandeep soon reached Hanuman Temple where a small crowd, especially of ladies, had gathered. Perhaps, it was the occasion of a festival. There were a few shops selling toys and sweets - a common sight in rural India. Sandeep stopped there for a while, watched the colourful gathering, and then walked towards Narrow Lane. He saw several groups of houses, almost touching each other, located on both sides of the street - some small, some large, some thatched, some made of bricks, and a few beautiful ones with large green lawns. That presented the scene of a mixed society, shared by poor and rich side by side. Even after decades of independence, the light of development was 50 kilometres away!

Sandeep walked the entire street, but he saw nothing unusual. *Why was he told to visit this lane in particular?*

Perplexed, he sat inside a tea stall. Soon thereafter, he saw see a youthful woman coming from a distance. She appeared approaching towards the stall itself, but she moved on. Her face looked vaguely familiar, but he could not remember how her image floated in his mind. *Was it an illusion?* he thought. Suddenly, like a flash of light, he recalled seeing a similar photo a few years ago. Gradually, the entire picture emerged in his mind. Shortly after he had passed the engineering examination, a proposal for his marriage, along with the girl's photograph, was received by his father. After consultation within the family, that photo was sent to him for approval. *That was this woman's photo,* he almost concluded; but remained sceptical too. At that time, he had rejected the proposal because he was unsettled in his career, and since then he has remained unmarried.

Some pertinent questions emerged in his mind: *Did she see my photograph as well? Should he meet this woman? Will it be appropriate at this juncture? Is she still unmarried?* His insight alerted, "In rural culture, talking to an unknown young woman is objectionable. Any such attempt could be harmful for the woman - even her character could be soiled."

He surveyed some parts of the village but could not concentrate because the youthful woman's picture appeared before his eyes time and again. He decided to return home intending to make a second trip next week. Before he could reach his car, a heavy rainfall and storm suddenly engulfed the area, and he took shelter in Sanjay's shop. The torrential rain continued almost for an hour that inundated all roads, caused flooding, damaged houses, and uprooted trees on the main road. The task of returning home became difficult for him, especially as darkness was approaching and driving a long distance was not safe in this weather.

Sandeep asked, "Is there a hotel or guest house in this locality?"

"You are talking like a foreigner. Have you come to a village for the first time? Had the village been so developed, you might not have come here!" replied Sanjay with a sarcasm.

Exasperated, Sandeep blurted, "Then tell me what to do? What's the alternative? Should I spend the night in my car?"

"Please, do not make me ashamed. If you spend the night in your car, how can I go home? You are a guest for the village, you have brought the dream of its development, then we also have an obligation." Sanjay said with humility and due seriousness.

"It's okay, please find a way out." Sandeep surrendered.

"For such unforeseen situations, Mukhiya ji, our Village Head, keeps an arrangement in his sprawling house for the visiting officials. If this arrangement fails, you will be my guest – I apologise in advance for the hardship." A smile appeared at Sandeep's face. He could not help thinking of the guy's sympathetic attitude, though he lacked genteel manners. *It was a symbol of rural culture!*

After a few phone calls, Sanjay received a message: "Mukhiya ji is away, but he has given permission to provide one night's accommodation in his guest room. Kindly bring Engineer Sahib and see that he is not inconvenienced. Does he have any food restriction?"

It was still raining, off and on, and the night was dark. Sanjay arranged a torch and an umbrella for Sandeep and a plastic overcoat for himself. On the way, during a casual conversation, Sanjay volunteered, "Mukhiya ji takes interest in politics and has access into higher circles. He frequently goes away on some assignments leaving his wife and daughter at home. His only son lives in London with his wife, they were married with fanfare two years ago. Perhaps, his daughter was also there for a few months doing a course."

"Did she go alone? Is she not married? Is her husband very busy?" queried Sandeep.

"It is rumoured that she does not want to marry, I don't know why. Maybe, she got influenced by foreign culture while she was in Britain."

Soon, both reached the destination. It was one of those large beautiful houses which Sandeep had seen earlier. They were courteously received by the gatekeeper; Sanjay Singh was relieved.

The guest room was in a corner of the main house, it was comfortable and well-arranged. Within ten-fifteen minutes, an orderly brought warm samosa and hot tea. Sandeep was already feeling tired and hungry, he enjoyed the refreshment. He picked up today's newspaper from the side table and busied himself.

Not long after, the orderly announced it was dinner time and he led Sandeep to the designated area. The wife of Mukhiya ji greeted him, "You are most welcome. I would like to thank the heavy rainfall which gave this opportunity of meeting with you. Perhaps, you have come to do a survey for the development of this area – please let us know without hesitation if any help is needed." Just then the telephone rang, Mukhiya ji was on the line. As a matter of formality, he talked to Sandeep for a few minutes and thanked him for coming.

"Dinner is getting cold, please start. And don't feel shy in eating. The food is vegetarian, it may not be up to your taste. You can have breakfast of your choice."

"Nothing like that, my mother also likes vegetarian food," he said, eating a piece of freshly cooked chapati. At that very moment, a young woman entered with a mobile phone in her hand, "Mummy, the sister-in-law is calling from London." Sandeep was amazed, it was the same woman he had seen in the daytime! The photo's episode again gripped his mind, he felt nervousness, and drops of perspiration appeared on his forehead.

Mrs Mukhiya ji introduced them, "My daughter, Sudha," and "Engineer Sahib from the district headquarters," and she left the hall with mobile phone in her hand.

Out of courtesy, turning towards Sudha, Sandeep said, "Please have something, the dinner is very tasty. Do you engage a regular cook?"

"I had my dinner just before you came, I will share the sweet dish with you," she replied gently. And then she observed, "By the way, are you feeling warm? I can see perspiration on your face, should I switch on the air conditioner?"

"No, thanks. The green chilly was hot and that caused perspiration. Now I am fine." At the same time, he realised that she was an astute observer.

Sudha picked up a magazine from the book rack. The silence became burdensome.

Breaking the spell of quietness, Sandeep enquired, "Do you also like vegetarian food?"

"I eat veg and non-veg both. But I have preference for fish which is healthier than red meats. The fish market was deserted in the afternoon because of heavy rains, so we have a simple meal tonight. What about you? Are you vegetarian or non-vegetarian?"

"I have no reservation, if the food is tasty."

Suddenly, a blast of wet air came through the window and heavy rainfall started again. Sparks from lightening also illuminated the room now and then.

"Have you phoned your wife? She must be very anxious." Sudha said innocently.

"Your anxiety is quite natural – it's a trait of women's heart. But I have not been lucky enough to have a life partner; I have already phoned my father."

"Your language has literary flavour - quite remarkable for an engineer. Perhaps, a symbol of emotional touch?" quipped Sudha.

Soon a helper from the kitchen brought a bowl of 'Gulab jamun', a common sweet dish. Before he could serve the guest, Sudha offered to serve it with her own hand. She placed two pieces in his plate, and one for herself. "It seems you are weight conscious." She did not reply.

"Gulab jamun is wonderful - we hardly get such a flavour in cities. Can I take one extra piece? Your mother did say 'no shyness in eating'," pronounced Sandeep.

Sudha could not help laughing. She placed two pieces in his plate saying: "One additional piece for your witty remark. You deserve a small prize, isn't it?" She seemed relaxed in the conversation.

"What about ...?" Sandeep stopped before completing the sentence.

"You stopped midway without completing the sentence, what's the matter?

"It could be uncomfortable for you, and, perhaps, uncivilised behaviour on my part. Showing interest in a young woman's life is always controversial, and I won't like to get into it. If you say something voluntarily, that will be another matter," he said politely.

Sudha spoke with magnanimity: "When meeting for the first time, one is always curious to know about each other, and perhaps this was also your intention – just natural. There is no question of arrogance or uncivilised behaviour and you should not worry. As you heard from my mother, my name is Sudha Varma. I am a post-graduate in History, and I take interest in politics – a gift from my father. I manage a non-government organisation which works for women's rights in this locality, especially in securing jobs for less-informed rural women. I believe job brings not only financial rewards but self-dignity also. Occasionally, I also become an honorary teacher in the local High School when the need arises. Just today, I got a call from the Head Master that two teachers suddenly went on leave and he sought my help. I engaged two classes to the benefit of students."

It was close to bedtime, she was summoned by her mother. She looked at her watch, it was getting late. She announced, "See you at the breakfast; good night."

"Yes, good night. And thanks for the hospitality."

Sandeep could not sleep well that night, his mind was caught in a web, and he changed sides several times. He wanted to return home at the earliest and search for that photograph to be sure that it was Sudha's. He wished to know why she had remained unmarried - anyone would be blessed to possess a woman of that calibre. *These were complex questions!*

There was a knock at his door: 'tea is ready'. The Sun had appeared over the horizon with full brightness; there was freshness in the surrounding; and farmers had already started going to their fields. At the breakfast table, Sudha's mother asked him, "Didn't you sleep well? Any inconvenience? Your eyes are still lazy."

Before he could speak, Sudha added, "It seems he was solving an old riddle. Where will he find such a peaceful place?" Sandeep blushed, what reply could he give? Soon after breakfast, he said, "I have an important meeting in the office, I have to hurry up."

"Next time, you can have lunch with us," Sudha invited in advance.

"I will keep in mind. Thanks for your very personal hospitality."

Sandeep was driving but Sudha's words were churning his mind: "'Riddle' can be anything, but what did she mean by 'old'? Did she use this word deliberately? Was she familiar with his name? Did she ever see his photograph? Did she recognise me?" Carefully, he reasoned with himself: *She didn't show any emotional upheaval or unexpected behaviour, rather she was very skilful and open. During a marriage negotiation, the girl's photo is often demanded but not of the boy. Perhaps, my father received Sudha's photograph from her father, but she didn't know. I didn't go to any studio during past few years, so the possibility of seeing my photo by her or by her mother did not arise.*

Sundeep's mind was in turmoil, the flame of excitement was burning his wisdom, and he was restless to find the truth. There were other dimensions too: he was greatly influenced by Sudha's personality, and most probably he had become a captive of the *unspoken attraction*.

Once at home, he thoroughly searched his almirahs, boxes, book racks, office files, and other nook and corners, but he did not find the photograph of any young woman. Perplexed, he spoke to his mother, "About there-four years ago, a few proposals for my wedding were received along with the photographs of the would-be brides. Are those photographs still lying somewhere?"

"Sensing your reluctance, some photographs were returned through the messengers itself; but some remained here because their sender's postal address was not available. They are lying in my almirah."

Finally, Sandeep found two photographs out of which one was Sudha's. He jumped with excitement – she has not changed much from those days! Natural attraction and equanimity were blended together in her expression. That removed one suspicion from his mind and he became fully assured that Sudha's photo was received for their wedding. But the second suspicion was still lurking in his mind: *Did she know about it?*

Another question arose in his mind: "Does the person, who had urged me to visit Narrow Lane, know that she lives there?" He phoned the guy, "I have returned after vising Narrow Lane, but I did not see anything unusual. Is there something special about that place?" The guy replied in detail: "Mukhiya ji lives there who has enviable contacts in politics. In the prevailing work-culture of our country, no major developmental project can proceed smoothly without political support. Hence, the support of Mukhiya ji at the local level is a necessity for our firm which has underwritten the scheme. Maybe, he has some expectations, but that can be shorted out later. I had thought that you would understand these intricacies while talking to the local populace."

"Thanks for your practical sense, I am still a novice. Because of very bad weather, I could not talk to local people as expected. Next time, I will take care and meet Mukhiya ji as well." Sandeep was satisfied.

Two weeks passed. Sudha read a column in the newspaper, "A major scheme has been approved by the government for the development of Rampur village and its adjoining areas. This project is being handled by a dutiful young engineer Mr

Sandeep Sharma." It was accompanied with his photograph. Delighted, she ran to his father and showed him the news. Seeing happiness at the daughter's face, he said, "Call him, and congratulate him on my behalf. This is the minimum courtesy expected, especially when he was our guest only a fortnight ago."

"But I don't have his phone number."

"I will find out soon."

Sandeep was in office when his phone rang. "Hello, Sandeep Sharma speaking."

"I am Sudha Varma. Do you have time for two minutes?"

"What a surprise! Yes, there is always time for you. I am alone in the office."

She said, "I have just read a column in today's newspaper that a major scheme for developing Rampur into a 'model village' with modern facilities has been approved by the government, and it will go ahead under your supervision. Congratulations for this, and my father has also conveyed his best wishes. You are a young, dutiful, and energetic engineer in the eyes of the journalist - what a tribute! Your photo is also attractive, don't let it be stolen." A sense of joyfulness was apparent in her voice, that could not remain hidden from Sandeep.

"You have added so many adjectives that I hardly deserve. Your photo is no less attractive!"

"What do you mean? Where did you see my photograph?" said blurted, being perplexed.

"It's in my mind," Sandeep spoke in a soft voice.

"Right now, please do your work. We can talk later." She disconnected the phone but remained mentally engaged.

Sandeep's heart beat became fast. What will he talk about, if she phoned again? Will it be appropriate to discuss about the past episode related to that failed marriage proposal? It was her father's duty to share that information; if he didn't, there must have been a valid reason. If she learns from me, how will she react? A debate was going in his mind. *He had heard the path of love was full of thorns, but it had already started pricking while the real love was miles away!*

He started working on the project with full attention, as if there was some unknown inspiration behind it. But he was alert – public support was also an asset in completing such projects. In view of this, his company wrote a letter to Mukhiya ji, "Before undertaking developmental works in your village, and the surrounding locality, my company wants to take the public into confidence by making them aware of the benefits. Hence, Mr Sandeep Sharma, the supervising engineer, and his associates would like to talk to villagers, and your help in organising a meeting will be greatly appreciated. Kindly arrange a venue on a suitable date and let us know at the earliest. It is desirable that the meeting is well attended by a cross section of the people."

That day arrived soon. The meeting was organised in a Primary School located in Narrow Lane, and the crowd was impressive. Mukhiya ji was himself present with his associates. Sudha was also present with a group of women, some from her non-government organisation. In a brief speech, Mukhiya ji welcomed all of them and invited Sandeep Sharma to give his presentation.

Sandeep, taking advantage of the power point display, explained the details of the proposed scheme in a simple language. Then he told the gathering: "I want to make it clear that your land may be acquired for widening the narrow roads, and even some houses can be demolished. But in each case, utmost care will be taken to minimise the hardship, give compensation speedily, and provide alternative plots for new abodes, etc. At the same time, there are many benefits: urbanisation will give a boost to your trades, new avenues of education will open, medical facilities will improve, more jobs will be available to local populace, contacts with external world will grow, economic globalisation will increase earnings, etc." Most of the people supported the scheme with clapping.

Sipping water from a glass, he said, "Now you may ask questions and put up your suggestions."

Sudha was the first to ask, "What provisions have you made for constructing toilets in homes? Many homes do not have a toilet - without it the dream of urbanisation is ludicrous. Have you ever thought about this? Leave aside homes, there are no separate toilets for girls in schools while their numbers are increasing fast. Your scheme is silent on this issue – how can it be a realistic model for the rural development?" There was a big applause, especially from women.

Perspiration appeared on Sandeep's face and the meeting's atmosphere became tense. Winning over his nervousness, he immediately said, "I have heard that you manage a non-government organisation which works for solving women's problems. You are welcome to give practical suggestions and we will certainly consider them. The truth is that this problem never drew our attention because we never faced this situation in our lives in cities. I am thankful to you, you have opened our eyes." A prolonged clapping indicated that he won the hearts of the audience. A thin smile surfaced on Sudha's lips - that did not go unnoticed by him.

Someone from a distant corner drew Sandeep's attention: "This village turns into an island in the rainy season, and it becomes dangerous for girls to cross the flooded roads for reaching High School. As a result, many of them get stranded in their homes. Can there be a solution for this problem? It's so important for girls' education."

"For a permanent solution, a bridge has to be constructed over the main water channel. As I have not assessed this situation, it is difficult to give a firm assurance until costs are estimated. Meanwhile, a boat can be arranged, and I will consult Mukhiya ji on this issue." People looked satisfied at this suggestion.

The meeting ended on a positive note, Sandeep passed a hurdle. Pleased, Mukhiya ji invited him for dinner. "Dinner will be inconvenient as I don't want to drive back in the night. I might come for the afternoon tea, if it suits you." "Why not? We will wait for you," said Sudha immediately.

As Sundeep entered the mansion of Mukhiya ji later in the afternoon, his face was beaming with confidence – it was but natural. Sudha welcomed him with a bouquet of flowers. "Why this formality? I don't deserve it. Bouquets are for famous people."

She explained, "It is not a formality, it's a symbol of honour which can be earned by anyone. Today, you have won the hearts of all villagers; what can be a greater honour? Try to keep your words of assurance – this bouquet will always remind you." She became emotional.

Sharing her emotions, he replied, "This is a rare gift for me, and a source of inspiration too. I will always see your image in these flowers." Mukhiya ji was standing by the side, he heard them, and was elated.

While sipping tea, Mukhiya ji asked, "When would you like to start the work? Any priority?"

Sandeep elaborated, "The time span of the project will be long, it might take years. In this process, our technical staff and other employees will keep on coming and going, and so will I for the supervision. Therefore, our priority is to construct a two-roomed guest house – one room for the office and the other one for night stay. A suitable site has already been selected and work will start very soon."

"The construction of your guest house might take months, where will you stay in the meantime?" Sudha enquired anxiously.

"It is not like that. These days, using pre-fabricated materials for a given design, a strong and reliable structure can be erected within two-three weeks. This type of construction is quite prevalent in foreign countries."

This technique can also be beneficial for villagers: Sudha imagined.

Then he told Mukhiya ji, "The rainy season is about two months away. I will appreciate if you can arrange a boat and one part-time boat-man, for which the entire cost will be borne by my company."

"In your company there are other partners, they may not consent. In that situation, bearing the entire cost from your own pocket can become expensive. Do you need help from the village council?"

"No, it is my personal assurance and I don't want to fail. In a sense, it's also my examination."

Sudha could not help saying: "It appears you are self-respecting as well! Where did you get this education from? I would be grateful to know."

"Self-respect or pride is not a commodity that can be purchased from the market, it's a way of life. It builds up gradually as life goes on. I have also sensed the same spirit in your personality."

"I am proud of you both. This perception will guide your future path." Mukhiya ji was moved by their thoughtful conversation.

"Now I would like to take leave, it is getting late." Sandeep got ready to leave.

Sudha came to see him off. "Next time, you have dinner with us," and she handed over a box.

"What's inside the box?"

"Gulab jamun," she said in a sweet voice.

"Thanks." A smile appeared on his lips.

The next day's newspaper published, in detail, what had happened at the meeting in Rampur village, and that included a verbatim description of Sudha's pointed questions. In the opinion of the journalist, that was a vivid example of women's empowerment which was a boon for democracy. The news column also included her photograph and laudatory comments made by others.

Early in the morning, Sandeep called Sudha, "Have you seen today's newspaper? Lots of congratulations! I wish you keep moving upward at the ladder of success."

"It was not possible without you. In fact, you equally share this notional prize," she said gracefully.

"I would like to cut this picture of yours and keep on my table. Do I have your permission?"

"Ask your heart," there was sweetness in her tone. She added, "There is one condition. No formality in the future, we can treat each other as friends."

"Yes, you are right. I had wanted to say the same, but I was hesitant."

"I am waiting for your next visit," she uttered impulsively.

One does not know what is fated: she closed her eyes.

The next six months were busy for Sandeep. Repair of main roads, removal of unauthorised possessions, widening of narrow streets, construction of government offices, etc were in progress. One technical team, with Sudha and two other women, was surveying homes for constructing toilets for which special grants were made available by the government. Sandeep regularly came, at least once in a fortnight, for supervision and he managed to see Sudha each time despite a busy routine; and she liked his suave manners.

It was her birthday when she received a congratulatory card from Sandeep. The card's inside had a beautiful picture of 'red roses' below which was written "I see your image in these roses". She pondered for a while, 'Why red roses?' A voice came from nowhere, "It is a symbol of love." She at once sent the reply, "You have become expert in symbolic language, I will try to comprehend." Looking for a document, her father entered the room and saw that birthday card lying open on her table. He read the written message, and thoughtfully made a conscious decision.

The very next week, unannounced, Mukhiya ji came to Sandeep's office when he was writing a report. He immediately stood up in respect and said nervously, "Is there something urgent? You could have phoned me, why did you take this trouble?" Sitting on a chair, Mukhiya ji said seriously, "Today,

I want to tell you a story. Listen carefully." "Ok, I must close the door."

Placing a photograph on the table, Mukhiya ji asked, "Do you recognise this photo?"

"Yes, why not? It is my photo taken at the convocation, when the Education Minister gave me a gold medal for securing the highest marks. How did you get this photo?"

"I was present in that ceremony. I was impressed by your qualification and personality, and I took a copy of that photo from the photographer. After a few months, I had sent your father a proposal for Sudha's marriage with you along with her photograph. As she was studious and beautiful, I thought that you would be a compatible match for her. But your father informed that you were not ready for the marriage, because your priority was career advancement. Sudha did not know about it.

"One day, I was discussing this matter with my wife when Sudha heard about it. The next morning, she said that she also wanted to establish herself in a career – if such a resolution can be taken by a man, then why not by a woman? A sense of new awakening engulfed her, a new confidence came in her personality. At that time, she was in the final year of her post-graduation; so, applying any undue pressure for marriage was not desirable. She is still on that path, and she is alone.

"The destiny has brought you both face to face. Both of you are qualified members of the younger generation, believer in progressive values, and competent to take decisions freely. Life's journey is long, it becomes easy with a companion."

Mukhiya ji left. The curtain of mystery disappeared, and Sandeep knew why Sudha had remained unmarried. *She was ambitious, dedicated, and resolute. The same traits adorned his personality – could they remain compatible?* He saw one ray of hope: *The seed of love had germinated between them, they will have to nurture this tender plant.*

In the following week, Sudha was seated before Sandeep. He asked, "Do you believe in destiny?"

"Why this question, suddenly? People talk about fate or destiny when an unexpected event suddenly happens in their life. I never had an occasion that persuaded me to think about fate. Of late, has any unexpected incident happened in your life?"

At that very moment, Sandeep took out a photo from his wallet and placed it at the table.

Bewildered, she spoke harshly, "Where did you get this photo? It is about three-four years old."

"Now, tell me whether it is an unexpected event, out of the blue, or a normal one."

"Don't create a mystery, tell me the truth. How did you get this old photograph?"

Patiently, he told her the entire story as enunciated by her father, and then mentioned how and when he found her photograph in his house. "Seeing you in Narrow Lane, facing rough weather, spending night in your father's home, meeting you at the dinner – all seem to be connected by a pre-planned chain. So many fateful, interconnected, events can't happen just by chance or through mere coincidence! If this is not a game of destiny, then what is it?" Sandeep put forward his views logically.

Sudha remained quiet for several minutes, a debate was going in her mind. Sandeep did not disturb her - he knew what happens when ideas clash in mind. Taking a deep breath, she spoke herself, "If this is destiny, as you say, then what's its purpose? What will be its consequence?"

"This is the paradox: *fate is inscrutable, unseen and unpredictable*. The existence of destiny cannot be proven by logic, it's a matter of the person's psychological state. If you are curious to know the end-result, ask your heart - not the mind."

She argued, "If our meeting was destined, then what about the invisible bond between us? Is it also a manifestation of the so-called inscrutable fate? Our mutual attraction has been noticed by my parents; then only my father told you about the past episode. Are our day-to-day activities also guided by the fate you believe in?"

"Saying so would be an exaggeration, perhaps ridiculous as well. The feeling of mutual attraction was a natural consequence of the *meeting of two minds*, it did not suddenly grow in one day. The elements which proved powerful included our education, dignity, intellectual grasp, resolution, professional behaviour, and mutual trust over a long period of time; bringing fate in these matters is not logical. Destiny provides an occasion in life, it does not decide our everyday rituals. One day, you gave me a box of 'Gulab jamun' – do you remember? That box contained the seed of unseen love, and that influenced me." Sandeep became sentimental.

"We can move ahead on our chosen paths and be successful, while nurturing the unseen bond between us – the so-called love in your eyes. What indication was given by my father?"

"Yes, we can move ahead. That will be like moving on two parallel trainlines, which merge into infinity but never meet. Life span is limited, and its meaningfulness lies in coming together – that was the message in your father's observations."

"You are talking like a philosopher. Explain in a simple language."

Sandeep gave a short speech: "Love has myriad dimensions, many facets, many interpretations. It is unseen, unspoken, internally blissful, and subjective in nature. It travels to your heart, bypassing the argumentative mind. Our love falls in that category, which you must have realised. Love is not an object that can be touched, it is imageless and abstract. We can feel its sensation and life-giving energy only after we embrace it. Just imagine a food – you cannot relish its taste unless you eat it."

Sudha posed a straight question, "What is the concrete form of love? How can one experience it?"

"Love is manifested in the form of intimate relationship – I can't explain further."

"Any means to measure the depth of love? Any credible proof?" she insisted.

"This question is difficult. I will try to answer, but don't consider me uncivilised if you feel hurt."

"In that case, I will ignore it for one day," she replied apprehensively.

Hesitatingly, looking into her eyes, Sandeep said, "The depth of love lies in the warmth of a man's kiss and the strength of his embrace. Women understand it intuitively."

"You are shameless!"

"Are you sure? Say it once more."

Sudha kept quiet. She blushed and closed her eyes.

Sandeep kissed her hand. She did not protest!

(Mukhiya = elected village head, ji = suffix used as a mark of respect)

6. New Destination

The express train to Jaipur was going fast. The night was dark, it rained intermittently, and the sound of occasional thunders was barely audible inside the airconditioned compartment. The outside world was hardly visible in the nightly darkness, except a few dwindling lamp posts when the train passed through small stations, but the compartment's interior was brightly lit and passengers in general were friendly. Anushka and her friend Priyanka were going for taking admission in an engineering college, which was like a milestone in their career. One needs to pass a tough competitive examination at the national level for a limited number of seats in engineering and technological colleges, and therefore getting selected for a reputed institution is like winning a coveted lottery.

On the seat opposite to Anushka, a smart young man, with a thin layer of nicely-cut attractive dark beard, was reading a magazine which flashed the picture of a famous Bollywood actress on its front cover. Anushka also held a book in her hand, but she looked at the magazine time and again. When her eyes met the youth's eyes once or twice, she turned her face away.

"Perhaps you want to see this magazine," said the young man offering her the magazine.

"No, there is nothing like that. My book is also interesting."

"Please don't be shy. The journey is long; we have plenty of time to spend on this train. In the meantime, I can peek into your book."

Anushka fixed her gaze on the cover page as if she was searching for something special. The picture had all that a young woman aspired for: ocean of beauty, intoxication of youthfulness, lover's paradise. She thought: '*Was it a lively woman's picture? Or the imagination of a poetic sculptor? If she is a model in flesh and blood, could I meet her?*' She was an amateur painter, she had won at a state-level competition, and she liked to pursue painting as a career. But because of the parents' pressure, she had to change her priority. Forcefully, they argued: in the modern digital age, it is the technical education that could enable her to be the master of her life through economic independence and social prestige. She succumbed to their arguments.

She was still in a pensive mood, when Priyanka grabbed the magazine. Seeing the picture, she jumped with surprise and blurted, "It's Sonalika! She was my sister's close friend in a public school in Delhi. She was talented and studious, but she took admission in a film institute after passing out from the school - ignoring the advice of the family members. She has changed a lot and become a celebrity. How come? And she looks gracefully innocent."

The man on the opposite seat heard what Priyanka had just said. He said, "I have heard what you said, and I could not resist from saying something. I apologise for this intrusion. After two weeks, the shooting of a film is planned in Jaipur and Miss Sonalika is playing the role of the main actress. Both of you can meet her, she has great respect for her friends and their intimate ones."

"How can you help us? Do you know her?" asked Anushka.

"I am the technical director of that film. I told you so in view of your keen interest in Miss Sonalika. After all, our films become successful with the support of the younger generation like you. If you happen to meet her with my initiative, I might also be benefited by gaining her sympathy."

"You are very clever. You want to take advantage of our short meeting."

"It is just a matter of chance. This much selfishness is acceptable in the movie world; you will realise it once you step into it," the young man said casually. Then he gave his business card to Anushka and scribbled the schedule of the shooting on a piece of paper.

Anushka read: Dinesh Sharma, Technical Director, Bhagawati Films, Phone No. 98005 23460. Intuitively, she asked, "What made you think that I might step into the world of movies? What did you mean by that?" She said with a bit of bitterness.

Dinesh explained in a disciplined manner: "Globalisation has changed the face of every profession, including industry. Every profession is becoming short-lived, one dimensional education is proving incomplete, people are being forced from one type of job into another, and this process is likely to accelerate with the arrival of the digital technology. Who knows – you may have to face the same. If this ever happens, please do remember that film production has become a global industry, it is no longer simply a means of song and dance. Indian films have established their powerful presence at the world platform."

Priyanka intervened, "What type of degree have you acquired? You have lectured like a professor!" Her tone was satirical.

"I appreciate your satirical comments, nothing unusual. I am a graduate in computer science and I have worked for two years as a programmer in a technology firm. These days, computers are playing a much greater role in film production – you must have seen animation films. The same technology is swallowing the film industry; that day is not far off when heroes and heroines would be unreal."

"This is not a pleasant news for the younger generation, their ambition can be thwarted," responded Anushka with anxiety.

Dinesh pleaded again: "You have taken a literal meaning of what I said, but it is not like that. Human emotions – love, affection, pleasure, excitement – can be truthfully demonstrated through live characters only; otherwise films might become a readymade stuff like tinned Indian spices or garments. Soon one gets bored by their use, as all of us want novelty. Human intervention is essential for new ideas, and the same is needed in the field of computers. That's why new programming tools and soft wares are cropping up almost every year."

Suddenly, Anushka enquired, "Can film industry be useful for me?"

"Your face is photogenic, it reflects natural attraction. Film producers are in search of such lively faces; *you can become a celebrity*. Now women born and brought up in the Western world are also eager to advance their career in Bollywood, and some of them have reached at the top. Such films can become a powerful vehicle for spreading the essence of Indian culture at the global level."

Priyanka interjected, "Our cultural ambassadors are those literary figures who have preserved our heritage through their scholarly writings since ages. Films, especially Bollywood movies, are known to provide cheap entertainment through their colourful, and often provocative, scenes. The impression created by such commercial films is transitory at best and their central motive is minting money. In fact, they seem too superficial and far away from the social reality."

Dinesh was overpowered by Priyanka's thoughtful perceptions. He responded carefully: "Whatever you have said cannot be disregarded. The conflict between literary figures and script writers, particularly in the use of language, is well known. Some scholars strongly believe that Bollywood movies have lowered the standard of Hindi language and diluted its eminence. On the other hand, such movies have also brought their writings closer to the masses and popularised this language. In recent times, Bollywood has played a significant role in projecting Hindi at the global level; in fact, more people have been drawn towards Hindi because of Bollywood films."

Suddenly, Anushka raised another issue. "What is your opinion about the sexual exploitation of girls in the glamorous world of cinemas? It is a sensitive issue for them."

"There is a difference between sexual exploitation and pre-marital or consensual sex, though the line of demarcation between them is dwindling. The exploitation in any form, whether physical or mental or economic, is deplorable; but that may not be the case all the time," said Dinesh in a guarded, but convincing, manner.

He continued: "A recent survey in Australia has indicated that about fifty percent of the girls leaving high schools had already indulged in sexual relationships. This cultural change has been facilitated by the advent of internet, Facebook, smartphones, etc, which have become ubiquitous and overbearing. These tools of the digital age have brought boys and girls, men and women, face-to-face – anywhere and everywhere including their workplaces and bedrooms. As a corollary, it has promoted physical attraction and sexual encounters wittingly or unwittingly. We do not have reliable statistics, but we are also proceeding in the same direction – after all the ghost of the Western civilisation has also affected our lives. Yes, its probability could be higher in the world of cinemas because an open and amorous surrounding works as a catalyst."

Priyanka became sad, she was not prepared for such an answer. Hesitatingly, she asked, "How can one remain unaffected from the evil influence of this emerging trend?"

"Every age has its own identity - it is coming from the time immemorial. As per Hindu religion, the present era falls within *Kaliyug,* which is synonymous with moral decay. We can call it the *flow of time,* which is hard to interrupt, but one can remain unblemished through self-control. When each section of society is feeling the pinch, the small world of cinemas cannot be expected to remain untouched. Of late, the mysterious life styles of the so-called religious *gurus* are getting exposed and they are facing charges of sexual harassment and misconduct." Dinesh appeared satisfied with his plausible arguments; he felt rather vindicated.

Priyanka, in a serious tone, said, "You speak like a philosopher: everything is destined, we are like human puppets. You might have argued: whenever there is a loss of *dharma,* Lord Vishnu's reincarnation takes place to re-establish those tenets. But what about ourselves? We can exercise control over our juvenile tendencies through the rein of wisdom and move on the righteous path."

Dinesh was astonished at the sharp intelligence and debating skills displayed by Priyanka. He could not help saying, "I respect your intellectual acumen and open mindedness."

Suddenly, Anushka enquired, "Are you married?"

"Why this question? It is a personal and private matter, and I would not like to respond. If the same question is put to you, how will you feel?"

Anushka wanted to say something, but the conductor providing service to the compartment came and said, "It is already late in the night. Kindly switch off the light and have rest, lest you annoy other passengers."

Anushka closed her eyes, but her mind was fully awake. The voice *"you can become a celebrity"* was resonating in her ears.

Priyanka had a dream: "You are the master of your own destiny." She couldn't sleep either.

They had spent more than two weeks in Jaipur, they were well settled in a women's hostel inside the college campus itself. They had already visited the "Pink City of Jaipur" more than once, seen its historical monuments, and enjoyed its foods. It was the spring season when this vibrant city had come to life with foreign visitors besides being adorned with natural bounties. The splendid ancient forts of the historical Rajput Kings mutely displayed their cultural and artistic heritage; the glory of Jaipur was there to realise.

It was Saturday, they had no classes to attend. Anushka phoned Dinesh Sharma and expressed their desire to watch the shooting of the film. "Yes, you may come. I will depute a person at the main gate to guide you people. Try to make it at 11 o'clock." The shooting was within the gated compound of a large fort famous for its well-preserved interior decorations and luxurious garden. Anushka and Priyanka were received at the gate and they were seated in a row reserved for the personal guests of the film producer. It was one of the best spots for watching the shooting.

On a specially designed stage, the main actors and junior partners skilfully performed their assigned roles under the glare of bright multicoloured lights expertly manipulated by technicians. The performance included pre-scripted dialogues, love scenes, dance sequences, background lyrics and music, etc, and their video recording from different angles by a group of trained photographers. Priyanka felt there was much difference between 'live acting' and 'cinema': projection on a screen appeared more attractive because of colour mixing and image enhancement with the aid of computers. She watched the performance with an analytical mind and imagined if she could become a part of the movie world! While enjoying the live acting, Anushka intermittently heard *"you can become a celebrity"* in her imaginative world.

About two hours later, Dinesh appeared before them. "Sonalika ji has to catch a flight to Mumbai and she may not have time to meet you people. However, she will soon appear for shooting in a swimming pool which is closed for outsiders. I can try to get permission for you people, but there is no guarantee. Priyanka ji, I recall you saying that your elder sister was her schoolmate – what was her name? Perhaps Sonalika ji remembers her."

Hesitatingly, Priyanka said, "My elder sister's name is Shalini. Sonalika liked this name very much – if possible, she could have changed her name to Shalini!"

Anushka interrupted, "Dinesh ji, please try your best. Our day will become memorable."

Soon, Dinesh returned with the good news: "Sonalika ji vividly remembers Shalini ji, and she has a soft corner for you people. She has arranged permission for both of you."

They, Anushka and Priyanka, saw an actress in swimming costumes for the first time – earlier they had seen in movies and Olympic telecasts. These days it has become feasible to edit photographs for the desired effects: a person's height, vital statistics, and physical appearance can be made more attractive by digital techniques. But seeing face-to-face produces a different impression and Sonalika was not an exception. In Priyanka's judgement, she looked much more glamorous and enticing in movies. Anushka had a similar opinion and she resolved to preserve her natural beauty, that was needed for the world of cinemas.

The swimming scene ended with an applause. Dinesh, Anushka, and Priyanka were walking along the narrow pathway around the swimming pool. Anushka was mentally engrossed; her high heel sandal slipped, and she fell into the waters. Dinesh jumped into the pool and lifted her in his arms. This incident happened so suddenly that no one had time to think what was right or wrong. In the meantime, someone captured this episode in a camera.

Almost after two months, Anushka received an envelope by post. It contained two pictures showing what had happened at the swimming pool; one photo showed her in Dinesh's arms in a normal conservative dress, but the second one showed her in a semi-transparent costume. In wet cloths, her blooming youthfulness was inviting to eyes. Fear stricken, she felt motionless, dumbfounded. Was it a dirty joke or a deliberate mischief? Was it a conspiracy to blackmail her? The envelope showed neither the sender's name nor that of the city it came from. She lost her sleep, she felt restless day and night. When Priyanka saw her pitiable condition, she inquired about it. Anushka showed her those photographs, shared her concerns, and broke down. Priyanka consoled her saying "we will face this challenge together" and embraced her; they sensed the warmth of friendship.

She added, "Whoever sent these pictures has become a culprit, and guilty of sexual harassment against women. The second picture clearly indicates that the sender or his collaborator is an expert in digital photography and computing. I am myself doing an advanced course in computer science and I am aware of its capability."

"Do you suspect Dinesh? Is he involved in this nefarious act?" asked Anushka nervously.

"No, are you crazy? It wasn't possible for him to shoot that photo when you were his arms. Also, did he know in advance that you would fall into the swimming pool? Had he known, one might speculate that he had hired a photographer for that episode!"

"You are right. I am losing my reasonings, Dinesh is above suspicion. I will let you know if something happens in the future. In the meantime, should I inform my parents?" said Anushka.

"It is hardly needed. Why to burden them with unnecessary anxiety? This is an era of women empowerment – we should have courage to stand up on our own feet," pleaded Priyanka forcefully.

"I should find out if Dinesh also received those photographs."

"Yes, that will be useful. But you should not phone him to enquire about this matter. If he takes up this issue, that would be a different situation."

Several months passed, but nothing unexpected happened. Anushka had almost forgotten the picture episode, when she received a letter from Dinesh: "I know you would be busy in your exams and after that you will have recess for five-six weeks. If you can manage to come to Mumbai during those days, that would be refreshing; and you might be able to meet Sonalika ji as well. The company of Priyanka ji would be doubly enjoyable." When Priyanka learnt about the offer, she casually said "will think about it later".

The exams ended as planned. Boys and girls started vacating their hostels; most of the girls had planned to go home. Free from tension, Anushka and Priyanka were taking coffee in the college canteen. Anushka started the conversation, "What have you decided about going to Mumbai?"

"I won't be able to make this trip as I have to work on an important project, but you should. You have artistic talents -

you do beautiful paintings - and you also have an inclination for the world of cinemas. This combination can work as a source of inspiration in your life, you should give it a chance to blossom. I remember the words *'you can become a celebrity'* said to you by Dinesh, and you haven't forgotten them. He had said so in the context of Bollywood, but you can broaden your outlook – celebrity does not mean becoming an actress only."

"What will happen to my studies?"

With a bit of anger, Priyanka argued, "What short of question is this? There is no reason to discontinue your studies – you are going to do a project, just like me. Nothing more or nothing less. Dinesh's letter has a similar indication, he wants to introduce you to a wider platform. You must use it to project your potential, consider it as an opportunity to move upward on the ladder of accomplishments. These days students often use their long holidays in learning skills in different areas like painting, pottery, sculpting, computing, swimming, sports, etc; and you are also going to give an expression to your latent talents.

"I believe that higher education brings maturity in thinking, proficiency in language and decency in behaviour, which are like the cherished ornaments in life. They are even more priceless for artists."

"You have opened my eyes. I will go to Mumbai and share my experiences with you." Anushka uttered with confidence, she had become motivated.

"Keep your eyes and ears open; you might be able to unravel the mystery of those pictures as well. And always listen to your inner voice."

"Of course. Thanks for your advice." A thin smile appeared on Anushka's lips.

It was late in the afternoon when Rajdhani Express entered the expansive city of Mumbai. Anushka had to get down at Dadar Central railway station, it was her first visit. She felt a bit apprehensive, she did not know what was hidden in the womb of this journey. Soon she got a message on her mobile phone: "I am Dinesh, will see you at the platform." When she got down, he came forward and got hold of her suitcase. "I can manage myself." "Just a helping hand. Be careful, your sandals might betray you again." They could not help laughing.

"A cup of coffee? You must be tired, it was a long journey."

She kept quiet. Dinesh bought coffee in two take-away cups and they strolled towards his car in the parking area. Soon his car was running on the Marine Drive – the most scenic road in Mumbai. The array of beautiful mansions on one side and the open sea on the other side presented an attractive sight when bright street lights came to life in the shape of a necklace. Anushka seemed enchanted, the opulence of Mumbai was in full display. She asked, "Where are we going? It must be very expensive to stay in this area, I will have to return soon." "Don't worry, you will stay in a guest house which is close to Miss Sonalika's residence. Visitors are provided accommodation in that complex which is quite safe. Breakfast is provided, but no lunch or dinner." After driving for an hour, Dinesh stopped his car in front of a restaurant.

They entered the restaurant, which appeared expensive at the very first sight, and were seated in a dimly lighted corner. The soft music was soothing, the atmosphere was relaxing and mildly aromatic.

"What beverage would you like to have? Fruit juice or coconut water or something else?" asked Dinesh courteously.

"I would like mineral water. You can take whatever is your favourite."

"And food - veg or non-veg?"

"I don't abstain from non-veg, but right now veg would be better. There is no binding on you."

Placing the menu card before her, Dinesh said: your choice will also be mine. Soon they were served by an efficient waitress.

"Cheese balls are tasty. It appears people in Mumbai are fond of savoury foods," said Anushka, "just like north Indians."

"Mumbai is very cosmopolitan and so are the restaurants. They serve to all tastes, you will have plenty of time to experiment with them." While taking dinner, they spent some time in little gossips that removed much of the formality in their conversation. "Miss Sonalika will see you tomorrow at 4 o'clock. Before that, it is your choice. If you need any help, don't hesitate to call me."

"I would like to see a few famous monuments, especially the Gateway of India and the nearby Taj Mahal Hotel - both are well-known for their majesty and history." Anushka said hesitatingly.

"I am busy, but I will send one of the company's cars. Since you have come to Mumbai for the first time, moving around all by yourself is not advisable. It is better that you have a woman companion as well."

He dropped her at the guest house. "Good night."

Anushka entered Sonalika's private office at the appointed time. "Come in, I was waiting for you. I am pleased that you could make this trip. And I admire your simplicity and natural beauty. What happened to Priyanka? Why didn't she come? Her elder sister, Shalini, was one of my best friends in the school; and presently she lives in the United States. When she comes to India, I would like to meet her," quipped Sonalika with a pleasant smile.

"Thanks for your courtesy and generosity. Priyanka is presently busy in a project, she might come here in the future. It was a sheer chance that we met Dinesh ji in a train, it was like finding a pearl in a deep ocean. One needs ability to bear a jewel – I have come in search of that." Anushka spoke with equal politeness.

"I can see a reflection of love in your language. Are you attracted toward Dinesh?" inquired Sonalika with surprise.

"No, ma'am. For me, he is not an individual but a cultural ambassador of Bollywood - and that includes you as well. I have come to unravel that hazy cover – the grandeur of the world of cinemas - from a close distance, and to realise its essence. It is also like a project for me, possibly it shows a new direction."

"There is depth in your thinking, and the wisdom of the younger generation. However, you will have to penetrate deep into the so-called haze and take part in its activities if you want to complete this project. Are you prepared for that? Think carefully - given your educational pursuits."

"Yes, I am ready," said Anushka confidently.

"Are you interested in any form of art – painting, dance, drama, etc?"

"Yes, I do paintings on canvas; and I have won a state-level prize too."

"Excellent! Our company is making a short film for school students, for which we need innocent young faces and you seem perfectly suited for that. It will be an educational film, not a commercial one. Through your paintings, you can bring into life the essence of rural culture and ecological well-being; it will also give you a chance to manifest your own perceptions. In this film of about 20 minutes you may be assigned 10 minutes and the rest could be taken by artists from other fields. Is it acceptable to you?"

Hesitatingly, Anushka said, "The proposal is praiseworthy, but I have an apprehension. These days, dirty pictures taken in disguise are circulated on social media platforms, and that becomes a cause of mental agony and sexual harassment. I am worried whether I could become a victim of this nasty trick and my image is soiled."

"This is the work of a few mischievous minds, it has no place in our industry. Bollywood has very strict rules; I can assure you of full protection from such misdemeanours."

"Then I am ready." A glow of happiness appeared on Anushka's face.

"I would like to tell you that this film is not for monetary gain, it is our social responsibility to produce such documentaries for the younger generation. However, my company will bear the expenses for your stay in Mumbai."

"I do understand." Anushka was satisfied.

After making two-three phone calls, Sonalika told her, "You can see the film director tomorrow at 11 o'clock in his office, and he will guide you henceforth. Of course, you can see me at any time."

The next day, when she entered the director's office, she saw three-four girls already seated in the waiting area and she also occupied one of the vacant chairs. Soon a spectacled, grey-haired, formally dressed, teacher-like grave, person appeared from an adjoining room and announced, "Anushka, come with me. I am the film director." She was astonished: *how did he know her.*

The director's chamber was artistically decorated and impressive. He occupied the leather chair on one side of the shining office-table and Anushka was seated on the opposite side. She heard a voice: "Look at the television screen, there is a video clip." She was puzzled – it was the recording of her conversation with Sonalika!

The director said, "I know you are astounded. This video is the property of this office, and Sonalika knows it. There is not much to ask, you are psychologically capable of handling the job. I am confidant you can work with our team and your talent will get a chance to flourish. Your training starts this afternoon and my office will remain in touch with you."

Before Anushka could say something, the director left his chair saying: "I have to attend a meeting." "Thank you, Sir." She had passed the first exam, and she felt encouraged.

For one week, Anushka remained busy in getting familiar with the techniques of film shooting and practicing myriad aspects of acting like a student of the film institute. She learnt about stage performance, emotional manifestations, facial makeups, dialogues, dance, background music, regular exercise, physical fitness, etc. And she spent several hours each day in watching live shootings so that she could digest some of the intricate points of film production. She realised that one needed inner resolution as well as practical efforts for manifesting one's latent potential.

Today, she was again in front of the director. "Your progress report is before me, everyone has praised your dedication and practice. You have passed the first stage and you need to continue regular practice for moving upward on the ladder of success. Acting is like meditation which demands full obeisance; I hope you find some time from your studies."

"I will try my best," she assured.

"In the coming week, you will practice acting for half-days and then work on a few paintings for the proposed film. One round of shooting will also be undertaken with school children and villagers in which you will play the central role; I will oversee the performance."

"Can I write something for the dialogue? I know this is usually done by accomplished script writers, but I would like to give it a chance," uttered Anushka with curiosity.

With an inscrutable gaze, the director responded: "You are ambitious, and I respect your intelligence. I had heard the videoclip of your conversation, its linguistic quality was commendable. I would be happy to discuss your proposal with the script writer, but I can't give you any assurance." "That much favour from you would be a boon for me."

For the next few days, Anushka painted several scenes which captured the natural beauty of the countryside, and the images of their iconic festivities. The mixture of vibrant colours under the guidance of the director made those painting lively, realistic, and attractive. She also gave a draft to the script writer: "Mother Nature has ensured the survival of humans since ages, and we have learnt to live in her benign shadow. The great pillar of civilisation needs a firm base which is embedded in her lap. Hence, the preservation of natural habitat is our sacred religion - a universal message for this generation. We must not forget that villages were our cradles and homes in early stages, and they are a part of our heritage. We must preserve this bond like an eternal priceless gift."

"In a few words, you have brought alive the soul of the proposed film. Congratulations!"

"Thanks for your appreciation," she spoke with humility.

The shooting of the film was completed in about three weeks. Before returning to Jaipur, Anushka came to say goodbye to Sonalika. She was welcomed: "How was your experience? Did you learn something from the world of cinemas? Perhaps, we can also learn from your suggestions."

Thoughtfully, Anushka replied: "Movie world is a meeting ground of multidimensional talents, not simply a platform for song and dance. But it is also true that glittering dances and seductive scenes have become the backbone of most of the films, which attracts people to the box office. If such scenes are curtailed, most of the movies might run into a monetary loss. In my opinion, Bollywood should move forward with the digital technology which has already overpowered the younger generation. Internet and smartphones have spread far and wide - even in villages and remote areas – and this provides an incentive for producing short artistic films that can be easily downloaded. In this manner educational and socially relevant films can be accessed by people at large at nominal costs, and this will also bring respect to film producers. Movie world can become a powerful partner in fulfilling national missions in different areas including cleanliness, sexual harassment, gender equality, corruption, etc."

"I will keep your suggestions in mind and we will remain in touch," Sonalika said gracefully.

"Thank you for your hospitality, I am deeply indebted."

When Anushka stepped out of Sonalika's office, she saw Dinesh approaching toward her. "You are leaving tomorrow. Tonight, can we have dinner together?"

"Yes, why not? I was also thinking of the same."

It was early evening. They reached a reputed hotel and were seated in a dimly lighted corner. Dinesh ordered for fruit juice and cold drink, and some light snacks to start with.

With apparent curiosity, Anushka enquired, "When will the film be ready?"

"It will take a few months, you will be informed. I understand your curiosity - it was also your test in a sense."

Dinesh continued talking: "I would like to say something, and unburden my mind, when you are going back. Months ago, I had received two photographs which showed both of us in an awkward situation. They were related to the occasion when you came to watch the shooting of a film in our Jaipur studio. Someone had mischievously taken a quick shot and made it salacious – rather revulsive. I suspected the person must be an expert in digital photography. As I am well-versed in computers, my needle of suspicion pointed toward one technician; and I kept a watchful eye on him for several months. Whenever he crossed my way, he avoided seeing me face to face. When we met in the office, he found an excuse to leave early. This was enough to conclude that he was the culprit, and I dismissed him. There is no place for such miscreants in Bollywood or in the wider field of entertainment industry. I thought I should make you cautious and alert. If you ever encounter such mischiefs, do not hesitate to inform me. Protecting your honour is our utmost priority."

Anushka kept quiet. Dinesh was trying to guess what was in her mind, when she abruptly changed the subject saying, "Let us behave like friends – that's more important."

"Yes, you are right." Dinesh had no time to think why she said so, but it ended the seriousness of the atmosphere. They could not help laughing.

"Now we should leave. Tomorrow, I have to get up early."

When they reached Mumbai Central station, the Jaipur-bound train was standing at the platform. Anushka walked fast. Dinesh lifted her suitcase and followed, saying "your sandals might play mischief again!"

Anushka occupied a window seat in the train. She waved to Dinesh and uttered: the name of my next film will be *High Heel Sandals*.

"What does it mean?" Dinesh was puzzled.

"Ask those photographs!"

Before he could respond, the train moved and picked up speed. He kept on looking, engrossed in a web of thoughts: *Did she receive those photographs? How did she feel if she saw them? Or somebody else told her? Despite that she remained calm, gracious, and devoted to work! An icon of self-confidant women!*

That night, he dreamed: Anushka stumbled from a ladder and he caught her in his arms. He woke up nervously, remained bemused. *It happens in films; can it happen in real life?*

It took six to seven months before her film *Dance with Nature* was released. Anushka's acting was highly rated, she became famous overnight. For the next two years, she spent her long holidays in Mumbai and acted in two short films *Climate Change* and *Women Empowerment*. Reports of her skilful performances were published by several magazines, but she was yet to appear on their front cover. Soon her studies were coming to an end, and it was time to think for a professional career.

On the other side, Priyanka was highly impressed by Anushka's success in films. For the last one year, she was also working part-time for an advertising firm where there was much demand for animation techniques. Several short videos produced by her had already appeared on television channels.

It was one of the days when Anushka was immersed in a knotty conflict. She told Priyanka, "I shall be facing the tough examination of life after a few months; I am confused like a man standing on an intersection not knowing which path to take. I see the degree of engineering on one side and the attraction of Bollywood on the other – diametrically opposite. What to do?"

Priyanka argued: "There is no inherent contradiction between the two, they can complement each other. I have seen your short films; your analytical mind, which is the product of your education, lies behind their success. You are smart and beautiful; these added qualifications will ensure smooth sailing in Bollywood. I would like to remind you that *beauty is the slave of time, but technical qualification is not.* If you feel bored or neglected in the world of cinemas, you can choose the other path."

"What have you planned for yourself?"

"I have received an offer from an American company which makes animation films, and I have decided to accept it. Animation is a digital art which is being used in different fields – from cinema to politics. Short and low budget animated films can be produced within a short time and marketed globally on the internet. This is the need of the hour - especially for the smartphone-savvy younger generation."

"Perhaps we can work together in the future to the benefit of the movie world." Anushka said enthusiastically.

"Why not?" Priyanka was supportive.

After three years. Bollywood was holding a function in Mumbai to celebrate the contribution of emerging young artists in the realm of cinemas. Priyanka was present as an invited guest; she had already achieved recognition for producing short animation films. A few weeks ago, an American magazine had published her picture on its front cover as well. In her speech, she said, "There is no dearth of multifaceted talents in young artists; there is unprecedented influence of modern technology in their ways of working; and they are a part of the global team transcending regional boundaries. The integration of man and machine has become a reality, and it is bound to produce changes in human behaviour. It's like the flow of time which cannot be restrained, better to accept it and use it in a productive manner. I see animation films from this perspective." The audience fully supported her through prolonged clapping.

She continued: "I have produced a short animation film which has not been released. I will inaugurate it here in the hall." Soon all the lights were switched off, people's eyes got fixed on the large screen at the podium. The film ran for about twenty minutes. After lights were switched on, she asked, "Who is the heroine of the film? Can you tell me?" There was silence for a few minutes, then someone said "Anushka ji." Anushka was sitting in the front row, the audience cheered her. Priyanka came forward and hugged Anushka. Photographers became active, their flashlights illuminated the hall.

A voice was heard: "Anushka was in Mumbai all along, how could she become the heroine?"

"This is the miracle of animation, a digital technique. That time is not far away when electronic characters will replace live humans in movies or elsewhere." Priyanka was prophetic.

The following week, a reputed film magazine's cover showed Priyanka and Anushka in a glamorous setting. And they were honoured with the words *"Celebrity of Digital Age."*

7. Turmoil in Heaven

(Place, Setting, and Background: The kingdom of gods – the heaven – and its grand auditorium. Indra, the king of gods, is seated on his golden throne on a raised platform; and four similar golden chairs are lying unoccupied – two on the left and two on the right side of the throne – for the special guests. About 20 -25 gods have occupied their seats; several orderlies are attentive towards the throne; and security guards are alert all around. There is curiosity among the attendees - the resident gods - as this meeting has been called by the king at a short notice without circulating any agenda. Soon a voice 'the meeting starts now' comes from the backstage; and the auditorium's curtain goes up. The attendees stand up in honour of the king Indra, and silence prevails.**)**

Breaking the silence, the king Indra said: I welcome you all. This meeting has been called at a short notice which might have inconvenienced some of you; I am sorry for that.
Many gods spoke at the same time: O merciful king! Showing regret for our inconvenience is a sign of your greatness and sensitivity, and we all are grateful for that. We are perturbed that no agenda has been circulated in advance, which is quite unusual. Are we facing any crisis or any impending danger?
Indra: There is no cause of anxiety, please have patience. Today's meeting has been called at the request of our venerable guests, and I do not have any idea of their complaint or discomfort. They will be here in a short while; in the meantime, you can interact with fellow gods and enjoy the heavenly drink s*om-ras*. (They mingle among themselves, chat casually, holding drinks in silver glasses.)
Not long after, a security guard announced: The most honoured Lord Shiva, Lord Vishnu, Lord Krishna, and the creator Brahma have entered the arena in their distinctive vehicles.

(Hearing this, Indra rushed to the auditorium's door to receive them; other gods followed him.)

King Indra: O venerable, you are most welcome. Kindly be seated and enhance the prestige of the gathering. (Lord Shiva and Lord Vishnu occupied the chairs kept on the right side of the king's throne; Lord Krishna and the creator Brahma occupied the chairs on the left side of the king's throne.) O Lord Shiva, the most venerable in the gods' clan! If the meeting starts with your opening remarks or suggestions, that will be most auspicious.

Shiva: O Indra, the king's words are like a command; I won't ignore your request. Do you know that unprecedented adverse changes are taking place on the earth? I am worried at that scenario.

Indra: My spies always keep an eye on the earth, but they have not reported anything unusual or extraordinary. I also know that many of the heaven's respectable residents land on the earth for enjoying holidays; in the same way as the earth's residents go to Kashmir, Switzerland, America or Australia as tourists. They have been making such trips throughout the year since centuries without any inconvenience.

Shiva: King Indra, whatever you have said is right. The natural bounties of the earth are extraordinarily enchanting, refreshing, and invigorating. Parvati and I also like to reside on the snowy terrain of Kailash mountain, high up on the Himalayas, during the summer season. You know that Parvati is called the daughter of Himalaya, and therefore that place is like a pilgrimage for me!

Indra: Then, any reason for complaint? Did some rascal interrupt your peaceful stay there? Or misbehave with you? My weapons will simply kill him. O venerable, kindly remove my suspicion.

Shiva: Hey Indra, please listen to me carefully; mental agitation dwarfs the rein of wisdom. I can't tolerate the excessive heat of the summer, and therefore I meditate on Kailash mountain covered with a clean white sheet of snow and relish the emptiness of the infinite universe. In between, I perform *tandava nritya,* the celestial dance, which spreads beneficial energy within the solar world. This time, I found the atmosphere was polluted, snowfall was limited, ill-effect of global warming was visible, and footprints of humans were in plenty. I also saw empty cans of Coke scattered here and there and felt the foul smell of urine at some places. Hence, I am angered, and I feel compelled to open my *third eye* which can bring destruction on the earth.

Indra: O merciful, kindly have restraint on your rage, otherwise the entire humanity will suffer from untold miseries. You had consumed the venom that came out from the churning of the ocean and saved the world from ferocious demons – then how can you become an instrument of destruction now? Please have some *som-ras*, the drink of gods; this will be soothing for your mind. In the meantime, I shall be consulting Lord Vishnu. (Soon, Indra is seen talking to Vishnu in a low voice.)

Vishnu: In a relaxing mood, I usually travel in a lotus-like fine boat with my wife, Laxmi, and move carefree through the entire Indian ocean. Even in deep slumber, I can visualise the beauty of the expansive blue ocean, the natural embracing of the earth and sky, the splendour of the sunrise into the distant horizon, and the unbounded intimacy of Laxmi. This pleasant feeling creates new energy in my body and mind, which helps me nurture the Brahma's creation.

Recently, I saw the movement of huge ships which tear the ocean's heart, pollute the environment, destroy thousands of underwater creatures, and disturb the natural serenity. I also saw pirates attacking ships and kidnapping crew members and heard the painful outcry of innocent passengers. I had never imagined such a brazen display of terror and highhandedness at the high sea, but it has become a reality. The fact is that I also became fearful and almost fled away in my boat; I broke my journey and returned to the heaven.

Indra: O omniscient, omnipresent, Vishnu! Your description has also made me fearful for a moment. But the heaven is fully protected, you can sleep undisturbed in a tranquil atmosphere. A glass of *som-ras,* the mythological beverage of gods, would be helpful. (At Indra's signal, a waitress serves beverage to Vishnu from a golden jar.)

Vishnu: Hey Indra, Lord Krishna seems eager to say something. His wisdom and experience would be most relevant; his knowledge is universally revered.

Indra: Hey Lord Krishna, the proponent of detached action and dutifulness! Kindly share your observations without delay; any waiting period will be painful.

Krishna: I spend my holidays in the hillocks of Vrindavan; I play on my flute and dance with young milkmaids. The supernatural tunes emanating from my flute overpower not only humans but birds and animals as well; they forget their existence and merge in me seeking eternal happiness. I feel elated and this gives a meaning to my benign presence on the earth.

In my recent visit, I found that my flute's overpowering effects were mostly lost in persistent sloganeering, noisy milieu, and the ear-piercing sound of loudspeakers. The milkmaids were not visible, they were afraid of kidnapping! I am anxious what could be the fate of this social pollution? I imagine the situation is not much different in other parts of the country.

(A gloomy silence enveloped the auditorium after hearing this description.)

Breaking long silence, one wise god spoke: For this pitiable condition on the land of God's incarnations, there could be many reasons; but excessive population growth is one of them – perhaps the most important one.

Immediately, Indra asked: O Yamraj, the god of death, are you not doing your duty efficiently? Have you become lazy? Or, are humans moving towards immortality?

Yamraj: O king, humans have become very clever; it is difficult to catch them. I am alert, but the conditions are adverse. I would like to describe some of the serious happenings.

A week ago, I had gone to catch a merchant – his life span was coming to an end very soon. I saw that he was eating in a Macdonald's restaurant in a busy locality. My vehicle *the buffalo* could not land easily because there was no parking space. I circled in the sky several times and finally landed after skilful manoeuvring. By that time the fellow had left the place in his powerful car. Quickly riding on my vehicle, I followed him but could not match his car's speed; and he avoided being caught. Hence the life-span prescribed by Brahma could not be executed, he escaped death. In a sense the creator Brahma's rule was violated and I am extremely sorry for that. I don't know how to atone for that lapse; I have already filed a formal regret letter.

While returning from that trip, I succeeded in catching two persons – one of them was an old farmer guarding his crops and the other one was a sick woman lying in a semi-conscious state in her dilapidated house. Possibly, this could water down Brahma's rage.

O king Indra, I can mention about another incident if you permit.

Before Indra could respond, Brahma uttered loudly: Yes, Yamraj, you have my permission. I am the creator of this world and hence I am curious to know how my rules are working, how this world is progressing or changing.

Yamraj: Just two days ago, I was traveling to the terrestrial world on my vehicle when I saw an aeroplane rushing towards me at a high speed. I took a sharp turn to avoid a mishap and my carrier, *the famous buffalo*, also got scared; I could hardly manage to avoid a fall. I had no option but to return to our heavenly abode. As a result, I could not catch the person whose longevity had expired; and he is still alive contrary to the writ of the creator. I am ashamed and possibly guilty of the dereliction of my duty. I am dumbfounded, the rules designed by the creator are in danger. In such circumstances, the explosion of population is unabated; as if humans are moving towards immortality.

Indra: Hey Yamraj, do you have any suggestion for enforcing Brahma's rules in an orderly fashion? If any, we will give it due consideration.

Yamraj: If you permit me to use your *Pushpak Viman*, the godly space vehicle, the implementation of Brahma's rules can be ensured more effectively. This space vehicle is invincible, it can face any challenging situation, it is ….

(Yamraj was interrupted, he could not complete the sentence; Indra spoke angrily.)

Indra: Yamraj, what sort of suggestion is this? *Pushpak Viman* is the symbol of the heaven's king; people worship it; it cannot be used to catch a dead person's soul. King's duty is to protect life, his symbol cannot be a merchant of death.

(Just then an agitated security guard entered the hall to the surprise of many attendees.)

Security guard: O king Indra, kindly pardon me for entering the hall so suddenly. I need your permission to explain the reason.

Several gods spoke simultaneously: You seem quite nervous; explain the situation fearlessly. We are eager to know what you have in your mind.

Security guard: A human shadow has entered this arena moments ago; he was earlier caught by Yamraj presumably after his death. He has reached here seeking justice from Brahma, he is excited and accusing Yamraj of highhandedness. *Justice delayed is justice denied* – so I came running to inform the righteous king.

Indra: Bring him respectfully and assure him that he will get justice.

Human shadow: My salutations to king Indra. I am a resident of the earthly world and a scientist by profession. I was in a thoughtful state; my eyes were closed; my body was motionless; and I was mentally engaged in solving an important problem. During this very period, Yamraj imprisoned me thinking that I was dead, and brought me here. Several years of my life are still left, but Yamraj is not ready to accept it; this is gross injustice – like hanging a person without a proven crime.

Brahma: I assign a life span to everyone at the time of their birth itself, which is regarded as fated or destined. Death comes at the end of the given life span or longevity, and Yamraj executes this rule. My calculations show that your life span has expired; any claim to the contrary is frivolous. It is not fair to accuse Yamraj of any arbitrariness.

Human shadow: O creator of the universe! There is a difference in the clocks of the heaven and the earth; in other words, time passes differently in these two worlds. Perhaps, your knowledge of science is limited or not updated. The measurement of time interval is not absolute, it depends on the relative motion of the observers; which was postulated by the great scientist Albert Einstein and confirmed by observations. Our two worlds – earth and heaven – always remain in motion in the grand scheme of the universe; which is also true for countless stars and planets. It appears that the heaven's clock runs much faster than the earth's clock, and that's the reason of difference in our calculations. Several years of my longevity are unused as measured by the earth's clock, and hence it is my right to remain alive.

Brahma: I write the life span of any individual based on the heaven's clock, that is also my clock. I do not accept the science of the earthly world.

Human shadow: Sir, science does not belong to a given world; it is universal, it governs the entire universe. While writing my longevity, you had not mentioned that it would be decided by the heaven's clock; therefore, I should get its benefit – which is the way of jurisprudence. Also, since the growth of my physical body has occurred with time as perceived on the earth, its decay or death should also be decided by the same timeframe.

(Brahma goes into a pensive mood for a little while before responding.)

Brahma: I will constitute a committee to examine your case and make the final recommendation. Until that happens, I permit you to go back to where you have come from. Yamraj will make suitable arrangements for your return.

Yamraj: O revered Brahma, your command has put me in a dilemma. How will I calculate the time of a person's death? How will I enforce your rule on the masses?

Brahma: Hey Yamraj, please listen carefully. Death is a boon for helpless, old or sick persons; it is a godly means to liberate them from an unbearable inhuman condition. In respect of such people, you continue working with your judgment as ever. But those who are young, energetic, dutiful, and devoted to public welfare may be treated differently – give them the benefit of my decision. And remember one thing: exercise caution in respect of intellectuals, I don't want to be trapped in their complex arguments.

Yamraj: Sir, your orders will be faithfully executed. I am also influenced by the arguments of this human shadow, he seems highly intelligent and wise.

Indra: Hey human shadow, I would like to ask you a few questions before you return to the terrestrial world. You are a scientist by profession and therefore your assessment would be objective. Are humans progressing towards immortality? If they succeed, they can earn the aura of gods; achieve godliness – *the god-like status*. This makes me worried.

Human shadow: There is no standard definition of immortality and godliness, and hence it is difficult to give a straight answer of your questions. However, I will try to satisfy your inquisitiveness.

Indra: Okay, that's fine. But try to use simple language which is comprehensible to all gods. It is hard to decipher the underlying meanings of a scientific dialogue without prior training.

Human shadow: It is imperative to know the difference between 'knowledge' and 'science'; the former has a much wider dimension than the latter which is limited by proven experimentation. For example, the realisation of love, compassion, kindness, selflessness, vice and virtue, comes under the domain of knowledge; which are elucidated in *Vedas, Puranas, Upanishads* and other epics, and they protect innate human values. On the other hand, science is the father of machines, vehicles, computers, medicines, and other appliances which have made our lives comfortable. Just ten thousand years ago, humans lived as hunter-gatherers in jungles and mountainous terrains, but today they have reached a very high level of civilisation – all because of miracles of scientific achievements.

The developed man of twenty-first century is capable to establish colonies in outer space and reach out to other worlds – all because of technological progress. In a way, he has become an ardent promotor of 'science' and disrespectful to 'knowledge'. Today's global religions emerge from 'science laboratories', not from the writings of *rishis and ascetics* living in caves! By designing new drugs, man has conquered many of the debilitating and life-threatening diseases; this has significantly increased human longevity and the process is continuing. You may call it moving towards immortality, if you so like.

Vishnu: It appears that man is living a 'mechanical life' which has very limited space for emotional sensitivities, but he will soon get fed up with boundless comforts. A meaningful existence requires a philosophy and a purpose, together they serve as life-sustaining nectar. It is interesting to know what could be their novel form?

Human shadow: The purpose is obvious: long life and long youthful years. Living long with feeble or worn-out body of old age will be a curse, and therefore long youthful years are much desired. Attempts for the fulfilment of the two are in progress; scientists are busy in deciphering the mystery of body's rejuvenation. Today, I am seeing the heaven's residents: they are healthy, handsome, energetic, and long-lived. Why can't humans be like that? The science will fulfil that dream! Perhaps, that is the path for achieving godliness.

Vishnu: Hey human shadow, what you say shows a glimpse of vanity. Are you challenging the heaven? Or trying to soil its honour?

Human shadow: Sir, I cannot indulge in such arrogance. I was simply talking about the probable direction of the scientific achievements. Presently, it looks like 'science fiction' but that may turn into reality sooner than expected; as has happened with many scientific breakthroughs. Twenty-first century's man wants to enjoy all the comforts in this life itself, not in the next life.

From time immemorial, religious leaders have urged humans to tolerate painful conditions in the hope of securing viable returns in the next life, that is after rebirth. Such sermons have lost their appeal, which is the victory of science; now humans rely more on their own intellect and wisdom than on godly scriptures. By the end of this century, man is planning to establish a colony on Mars – this much indication is enough for the heaven's wise residents.

Vishnu: Heaven's culture is much different from that of the earthly world, and we differ in our perspectives. Though humans and gods behave differently, they respect each other. It is possible that humans achieve the so-called 'immortality and godliness' in near future; but what after that? Will they try to subjugate the heaven? And start new struggles?

Human shadow: O venerable Vishnu, this question is purely hypothetical; it will be decided by the future generation. However, I would like to say that struggles between civilisations had been taking place on the earth since ages, and they are continuing even today in the guise of religious conflict or economic exploitation. It is difficult to predict what would be their form and dimension in the future. We should remember that the fight between gods and demons for the 'pitcher of nectar' that emerged from the churning of the ocean was also a conflict between two cultures.

Indra: Hey human shadow, your deliberations have created turmoil in the heaven and compelled us to a new way of

thinking. Now it's time for your return and Yamraj is waiting for you.
Human shadow: Before returning, I would like to make a submission to Lord Krishna. Can I have your kind permission, please?
Krishna: Hey human shadow, I was carefully listening to your discourse. You can share your thoughts with me without hesitation.
Human shadow: Hey revered Krishna, you have given the mantras of dutifulness *'karmanye vadhikaraste, ma phaleshu kadachana'*; that is: you have a right to perform your prescribed duty, but you are not entitled to the fruits of action. The scientists of the earthly world are following the same precepts, and they are motivated by public welfare. Should they abandon their quest fearing that their discoveries might be misused? Had it been so, the world would have remained superstitious and much less privileged; perhaps not even capable of feeding itself. At this juncture, your guidelines would be invaluable.
Krishna: I know that twenty-first century humans are getting smarter, they are progressing rapidly. They are the father of self-working intelligent machines, and the creator of new visions. I am afraid such machines could become the master of mankind, this would be calamitous and destructive. The unification of man and machine seems plausible, but this may obstruct the evolutionary process of the past two hundred thousand years! Some distinguished scientists and thinkers have already opined that smarter artificial intelligence is one of the 21st century's most dangerous threats. It would be impractical for me to predict the full consequences of such changes.
Human shadow: I will convey your message and apprehension to the scientific community based on the earth. Another suspicion is arising in my mind. I can share it with all of you with the kind permission of king Indra.
Indra: Yes, please be quick. Yamraj is getting delayed.
Human shadow: Sir, women are not present in this gathering of gods. Is it a chance or the heaven's culture? Many goddesses

– such as Parvati, Laxmi, Sarasvati – are adored in the terrestrial world, but none of them are visible in this meeting. This is an era of women empowerment; an era of gender equality; then why not in the heaven? The Indian women are frontrunners in many fields including politics, administration and science; and they are no longer confined in homes. Has this message not reached the world of gods?

(King Indra's face becomes serious, he seems uneasy, and looks towards Krishna for help.)

Krishna: Hey human shadow, your words testify to the changing values of the modern terrestrial world, and they are worth emulation. The dignity of gods lies in embracing those changes.

Human shadow: Yes, Sir. Goodbye!

(Curtain comes down, the drama ends.)

(**Hints:** Literature is the mirror of society, which is the theme of this short drama. Its contents reflect the images of the twenty-first century – its burning issues, achievements, and questions. The language is satirical, imaginative, and thought provoking. The participation of godly, mythological, figures reminds us of our cultural heritage; they interact as humans though from a different world. It is a work of fiction, not to be conceived in a religious context.)

8. Changing Values

The New Year's arrival was in the air. It was the morning of the first day of January in Melbourne; a sense of agility, enthusiasm, and aspirations seemed to defeat the monotony of the yesteryear. Television channels displayed the amazing scenes of colourful fireworks beamed from across the globe, and live programs of dance and music anchored by celebrities entertained everyone free of cost. Children planned for a family picnic, and adults were not far behind – it was a day of celebration complemented by warm and enjoyable weather.

The winter season was on its peak in north India, with shivering cold and a thick layer of fog, and most of the people were compelled to remain inside; while children were feeling disgusted with the unkind weather catalysed by pollution and climate change. The heavy snowfall in Europe had left many people immobilised for the past one week with no sign of immediate relief and for them the new year celebrations were likely to remain ritualistic with little excitement. Conditions in North America were not much different, making new year celebration an indoor affair with exotic cuisines and drinks. On the other side of the globe, in Australia, it was summertime – most enjoyable for locals and visitors from all over the world - when the natural bounties of the continent show their grandeur and diversity in myriad ways.

Manish was still enjoying the warmth of the cosy bed when his mother yelled, "It is the first day of the new year, go to the nearby Radha-Krishna temple and offer prayers. And take Radhika along with you, gods feel pleased seeing husband and wife together. The Sun-god has a appeared above the horizon; you should salute him with folded hands – after all he is the saviour of all lives including humans."

How could his wife, Radhika, leave this occasion without a teasing complaint? She added, "I am telling him to leave the bed for the past half-hour, but he never listens to me. Mother-in-law, only you can give him orders – it is your right. Tourists in large numbers have landed in Melbourne, the most liveable city in the world for several years, to celebrate the new year, but Manish hardly cares. I have to cook some sweets and savouries also for the evening party at a friend's home."

Their son, Deepak, spoke excitedly, "If we don't go early, good picnic spots in the park might not be available. My friend's maternal grandparents are also coming for the picnic – I have just got a call from my friend. And we have also planned a short cricket game for which the weather is excellent – anyway, an Australian picnic cannot go without an outdoor game."

Manish was listening to all the conversations, he was fully awake though wrapped in a warm blanket; now he had no alternative but to join them. Emerging from the bedroom, he uttered, "Please get ready soon, we all will go to the temple. We can buy fresh flowers and sweets on the way."

His mother said, "I have got pain in my knees, I won't be able to negotiate the temple's stairs. Today, the temple will be crowded as well – it is an old tradition to do puja on the first day of the year. I can offer my prayers from here itself; God is merciful, He can listen to His devotees from a distance."

Hearing of the agony of his grandmother, Deepak offered, "I will stay here with the grandmother, how can she be alone? She might need some help. In the meantime, I will call my friends and decide on arrangements for playing cricket. Also, it would be desirable to have some entertainment – like listening to some melodious songs."

Soon Manish and Radhika walked towards the temple, about a kilometre away from their home, considering the difficulty in finding a parking space on a festive occasion. Manish reached the destination a bit earlier, while Radhika got delayed as she found a talkative friend on the way. Seeing her husband, she complained, "You reached timely walking with long steps, but I was left behind. And you are enjoying the temple's grand decoration, while I am wet with perspiration. It hardly appears a friendly gesture, especially on this day; I wonder at your manners!"

"I walked fast to join the queue so that we are not left behind in receiving blessings from the god. This is Australia where one stands in a queue for receiving any benefit, and this system is appreciated by officials. I thought that gods might be doing the same, no scope for backdoor blessings!" Manish's logic seemed to convince his wife.

Manish was ahead in the queue and Radhika was just behind him. They asked for blessings when their turn came.

Smilingly, Radhika queried, "What blessings have you asked for?"

"After taking bath and meditating before gods' statues each day, you often ask for health, wealth, and well-being of the family; that I have heard many times. So, I asked for something new," replied Manish in a lighter mood.

"Don't create a riddle. Tell me frankly in a plain language."

"O merciful god! Let my wife's face glow with Bollywood's lustre, and inspire her to observe silence for one day in a week." Manish spoke in a grave tone, emanating truthfulness.

"You are joking, becoming satirical. Temple is a place for abiding faith in gods, not a place for cheap jokes," she said angrily.

"I am telling you the truth; that is what I asked for. I do believe in the sanctity of the temple's premises, it's not a place for telling lies."

Puzzled at his thinking, she questioned, "What have you asked for yourself? An actor's youthfulness? Anything charismatic?"

Manish replied discretely, "Your one day's silence will not be less than a boon for me! I would be able to watch cricket, read books, write poems, and listen to songs – all undisturbed. Are they less than a pleasant boon?"

Radhika was flabbergasted, rather annoyed; she was in a rage. Holding her hand with love, Manish enquired gently,

"What blessings have you asked for? It is said that here one's wishes are fulfilled sooner than anticipated, which brings many devotees to this temple."

She blurted in a sharp tone, "Let my mother-in-law see a dream that she must return home soon – even after four weeks her return flight has not been confirmed. Other blessings I have asked for are: let your secretary be a matured lady, and your snoring be less noisy."

Manish was anguished, but he kept quiet thinking of the idiom *nahale pe dehla* - tit for tat. "Let's go home, it's getting late."

As they entered their house, his mother announced excitedly, "I have prepared gram-flour's laddu; Deepak has already eaten several pieces, you people can have too. Fresh laddus are more delicious."

"Yes, mother-in-law" and she went straight to her room. For one moment she encountered a question in her mind, "Did she ask for the right blessing?" But the next moment, the reign of wisdom lost its grip on her ugly attitude.

The very next day, Manish saw that Radhika was observing silence. He was surprised – she must have thought that her blessing would be fulfilled only after his blessing was fulfilled, because he was ahead of her in the queue. He self-reflected, and he felt defeated.

After two days, when he returned from the work, he found Radhika in a cheerful mood – her face was shining with satisfaction. She quipped, "Mother-in-law's return ticket has been confirmed, she is flying back next week. Let's go to the market, she needs a new suitcase."

Manish was dumbfounded: *Do gods really give blessings? And so soon?* Tonight, he could not sleep, he was engaged in self-debate: *Was it the god's blessing or a sheer chance?* He repeated this question several times but could not get an answer. As he could not sleep, he didn't snore that night. Radhika was overjoyed: *God was merciful!*

Whatever be the answer, this is a glimpse of the coming era. New generation wants freedom, it wants to keep away from the shadow of the past. Whether this story is considered a flight of imagination or a satire or a fictional plot, it is a mirror of the contemporary social reality. This image is getting more meaningful as we move forward in the twenty-first century.

9. Clever Man

An elderly farmer had been working in the field for the past several hours and he needed rest. It was late afternoon, but the sun was still strong; he wanted to lie down under the shadow of a dense tree which was at a short distance. However, it was a herculean task for him to carry the heavy bundle of the harvested crops on his head and reach the anticipated destination. He called his son on his mobile phone for help, but he heard a recorded message "Please leave your name and phone number, I will call you as soon as possible". Feeling angered, he disconnected the phone without leaving any message. Then he phoned his daughter-in-law who replied "I am breastfeeding my son, how can I come? Kindly spend some time in the field itself; the sunlight will become less scorching within an hour or two."

Frustrated and deeply anguished, he said to himself: "If my wife were alive, she would have come almost running and brought some snacks as well, but now I have become a burden on the family. I pray God every day to give me shelter in His kingdom, but He never listens. What's the purpose of doing so much puja and reciting His hymns? Perhaps, those who regard 'gods' statues' as mere stones – powerless and unworthy of any attention – are much wiser." Tears of grief fell from his eyes, he felt depressed. The wound on his lower leg, which resulted when a sharp tool accidently hit him a few days ago, was also under persistent attack by nasty bush flies. The herbal medicine did not prove very effective, and his pain had increased as a result.

Exhausted, he sat on the crops' bundle itself. After a while, he saw someone coming toward him; he was surprised – the field looked deserted, then who appeared suddenly? That guy moved fast, approached the farmer, and said, "I am *Yamraj*, the god of death. God is pleased with your puja and devotion, and He has listened to your prayer. If you come with me, you will get a place in the heaven and achieve salvation from the perishable earthly world."

"No, I have not asked for any mercy from the almighty God. You have come to a wrong place, perhaps due to misunderstanding," said the farmer.

"I don't tell lies. Just a while ago, you complained that God did not listen to your prayer for giving shelter in His kingdom. Is it not true?"

"Do you have a tape-recording of what I said? What proof do you have that proves your contention? Any witness?" Attachment to life was showing its powerful grip on the farmer – nobody wants to die!

Yamraj was puzzled, speechless at the farmer's arguments. He had never faced such a predicament, he felt defeated. Finally, he told the farmer, "Please tell me how to resolve this vexed issue. I would like to reiterate that I am telling the truth – I didn't suffer from any misunderstanding."

"There is one way out, if you agree. We may seek judgement from a court of law."

Laughing at this proposal, Yamraj said, "I know an enforceable judgement form the court of law in India takes decades; a dispute travels from lower court to supreme court before it is finalized. I don't want to fall in this trap, it will benefit the attorneys only. Since I have travelled from heaven to earth, and because I am a messenger of God, it is my solemn duty to give you a gift. Tell me, what do you want?"

"If you are so pleased, kindly alleviate the pain of my leg's wound. After that, I would be able to carry the bundle of crops and go home." The farmer spoke in a satirical language.

"But there is one condition: this will remain confidential. The moment you disclose what has happened today, the effect of my boon will disappear, and you will suffer from more pain."

"Yes, I agree," said the farmer.

Yamraj said "so be it" and he disappeared.

The farmer's leg became free from any pain! He was mesmerized and perplexed at what had happened. He repented at his discourteous manners, didn't know how to apologize to the godly figure who was nowhere to be seen. Silently, he thanked him for his blessings.

More than six months passed. The farmer had almost forgotten about his encounter with *Yamraj*, when he fell ill. Despite medical treatments and care, his condition did not improve – he became bedridden. He felt as if his life's end was approaching. Hence, he thought of *Yamraj* conscientiously, "Before dying, I would like to see you – it is also my last wish." Out of compassion, *Yamraj* appeared and asked, "What's the matter? Why did you reminisce me?"

"O venerable *Yamraj*, my life's end is very close. If I could know the timing of my death, I would be able to meet my relatives and friends to my utter satisfaction. Then, I would embrace death happily."

"Doing so will violate the laws established by Brahma, the creator. I can't tell you the time of your death."

"Maharaj, every law has some exceptions. Some people say: *exceptions justify the rules.* You may consider it as one of those exceptional circumstances and tell me in confidence; I promise not to divulge it to anyone – I am already bedridden and helpless."

At the farmer's request, *Yamraj* was moved. He said, "That time is exactly after twenty-four hours, and I will come myself to take your life's spirit. None else should know about it."

"It's okay. Please adjust the time in your watch with that in my watch, so that they are synchronized. I don't want to create any hindrance in your duty."

"I agree with your suggestion," said *Yamraj* and then disappeared.

The farmer's mind was wavering, it was the last night of his life. He had already met his relatives and friends; he was lying alone, and his eyes were fixed on the wall clock. He was carefully listening to the tick-tick sound coming from the clock;

he started counting each stroke as the appointed time was due to hit any moment! He was astonished that *Yamraj* didn't arrive while the clock showed five minutes past the twenty-four-hour period. How could it be? Just then, the farmer heard "Now only ten seconds are left, close your eyes and remember God. You can achieve salvation by remembering the Almighty during last moments of your life." Soon, Yamraj appeared before the sick farmer.

The farmer shouted in a loud voice, "Please stay where you are, don't touch me. Look at my clock, it shows five minutes more than the prescribed time. Your watch had gone slow while you were travelling at high speed; this is predicted by the Einstein's theory of special relativity. Today, a farmer with little education, has seen its proof!

"In our legal system, execution by hanging is withheld if not done at the appointed time. Then, how can you take my life? The justice system of the heaven, the world of gods, is revered; how can you transgress that?"

Yamraj was puzzled, he felt a dilemma. Before he could say anything, the farmer argued, "I am a resident of the perishable world, the earth, and therefore my lifespan should be determined by the local timeframe. If you wish, you may discuss this issue with the creator of the universe, Brahma; he is the one who decides our lifespan."

"What you say is worth consideration. I will raise this issue at the next meeting of gods. In the meantime, I give you an extension of life as a gift," quipped *Yamraj* and disappeared.

Soon thereafter, *Yamraj* told the gathering of gods, "The man of twenty-first century has become very clever, his life is guided by the achievements of science. He has become his own master in many ways, and the influence of gods in his life is dwindling. In a way, the honour of heaven is in danger."

This is the paradox. Man is becoming his own enemy, and the cause of mutual annihilation. The role of the creator, Brahma, is becoming irrelevant; life and death are often controlled by science, and destiny is losing its ground. The old philosophy based on the intervention of gods in life's pleasure or pain is dying. Mankind needs a new philosophy for its journey.

Poems

(Reflective & Satirical)

Poetry is like a bird, it ignores all frontiers.
Yevgeny Yevtushenko

1. Air of Romance

In a crowded morning-train
I saw your face
Which sent a silent message,
When the train applied its brakes
I touched you for a moment, and
Felt a strange sensation
That lies beyond my description,
When I looked into your eyes
I sensed a bout of attraction, and
Embraced you in my imagination,
Forgive me
For not seeking your permission.

My phone rang the next morning, but
The number was unknown
I cursed my boss, who
Often gives me strokes
At unearthly painful hours,
I hurriedly pressed
The speaker phone's button, and
Hurriedly jumped on the bed
On hearing a sweet melodious voice
"Join me for a cup of coffee
At the steps of Federation Square
Why to suppress the sprouting desire?"

Before I could ask for the fateful time
The phone went dead, but
A smile appeared on my face
I thanked my phone
Which had saved her number with grace!

I wondered: *how she got my number?*

Half-minded, I reached my office
But I was denied entry
Because my ID card was missing!
I smiled again
And thanked the card for saving my day!

I was bemused:
Was it love at the first glance?
Or a gift of the modern digital age?
Whatever be the answer
It's a trait of the new generation, and
A means of the life's celebration.

2. Lessons of Life

My wife said 'Morning tea is ready'
'Please, a cup of coffee for me' I ventured
'Sugar, and milk?' she queried
'Nothing, just let it filter
I like the natural flavour.'

She brought tea and coffee in flowery cups
They were sitting side-by-side in a tray
One looked pale yellow
And the other one had deep brown colour
I smelt their intermingling vapour
That gave a pleasing aroma
I pondered: *Was there a lesson in what I saw?*

There was a flutter in the backyard
It was our white rabbit and black doggy
I threw a piece of bread
They shared and nodded to each other
I pondered: *Was there a lesson in what I saw?*

I went for prayer in a Church
Where the pastor was giving sermons
Someone from the audience interrupted
'Bible, Geeta, Quran' each has five letters
Can you explain the reasons?
Soon came another voice
'Church, Temple, Mosque' each has six letters
Can I know their hidden message?
A third voice was even sharper
'Pastor, Priest, Mullah' each has six letters
Can you solve this mysterious puzzle?

As the Pastor was perplexed

I raised my hand and came at the podium
"It's God's dictum that all faiths are the same."
The audience agreed 'Amen!'

(Social symbolism: white, black, brown, yellow)

3. We Live Together

We live in a land of bountiful nature
And enjoy the fruits of composite culture,
We walk on its lands and dusty deserts
And love its golden beaches and oceans,
We call it the great Australian nation
And take pride in its age-old democratic traditions.

On any festive occasion
Be it Christmas, Eid or Diwali celebration
We embrace each other with friendly passion
Whatever be our religion.
This is a part of our religious freedom
And a solemn gift of several generations.

Sometimes we also argue and quarrel
Which is a part of the human nature,
But I get deeply saddened
When people fight with ugly swords of religion
And faith becomes a weapon of destruction.
I often wonder
Where goes the innate compassion
And the friendly bond of human relations!

Like ocean waves from all directions
We came here from distant corners,
White, black, brown, and yellow
Together we make a unique fellow.

When I ponder at the Godly domains
'Temple, Church, and Mosque'
I wonder *why all have six letters!*
When I look at the sacred books
'Geeta, Bible, and Quran'

I wonder *why all have five letters!*

Logic defies, science fails
At this very moment 'Unity of Faiths' prevails
It is time to share this conviction
As we are becoming global citizens,
Let us come together
And preserve the bonds of social cohesion.

4. Dilemma of Devotees

O Almighty God,
I want to pray in silence for your merciful attention
I want to share my feelings, my sense of devotion
And recite some hymns in your honour with passion,
I also want to tell you the stories of my awful tragedies
Which have shaken my faith in your latent blessings.
But how? And where?

In a noisy temple's atmosphere
I can hardly meditate and fix my gaze on your image,
The open trade of costly offerings
And gifts to priests are heavy on devotees
Who are often short of money,
The globalisation of rituals has many partners
Which include scholarly pundits and deceitful imposters
I find it hard to identify the truly wise ones;
In this prevailing confusion
O God, I humbly bow before your hall of residence
And offer flowers from a safe distance.

In search of You
I came running to a glamorous Church
At its door I faced numbers of questions
"Catholic or Protestant? Methodist or Uniting?"
It was difficult to pass this examination
So, I hurriedly left that destination.

Exhausted, I entered a nearby Mosque
Hoping to have a glimpse of Allah's grace
But soon I saw
A fiery quarrel between Shias and Sunnis, and
Covered my face in a dark space,
My heart pounded with fear

I managed to escape with the help of a believer.

Huffing and puffing
I reached a Gurudwara for peace of mind
Before I could enter
The security guard gave a cryptic command
"Cover your head with a turban
Or a towel or even with a handkerchief,
Else, your entry will be an act of mischief."
I loudly said "Satya Shree Akal"
And walked towards a local bazar,
I talked to myself
"Instead of realising the Godly bliss
I am wandering around for a cloth's piece!"

O Lord, I am perturbed today
Seeing discrimination in your holy domains;
When humans descended on the earth
They inherited a part of your traits
And You had planted the seeds of sublime love
Noble character and brotherly feelings in their being,
But the tender plants of those seeds
Got infected with the cruel disease of discrimination,
'How to cure them?' has become a big question.

O Omniscient Lord,
The devout preachers of all faiths
Sing devotional songs with full dedication,
But they fail to share the fruits of your garden
And mitigate the 'Dilemma of Devotees',
Humanity needs a global religion
That practices compassion without discrimination.

I wonder 'where to pray in silence'
The only place I find is my own inner space!

5. In Memory Lane

Nature's beauty came alive
When the spring season spread its wings
Full of energy in vibrant colours
Like a bride in her youthful years.

That infused energy in my tired veins
And sharpened my memories of yesteryears,
The lost images became visible
The sound of silence became audible
And my sterile senses became fertile!
I grabbed my pen, and
Captured them in black and white.

Who was she who sat on the nearby bench?
Taking shelter from the teachers' gaze
I often peeked at her charming face
And drew her pictures on a piece of paper
Soon I became a lonely painter,
I filled those pictures with colours of love
But never dared to meet her face-to-face!
I cursed our cultural manners, where
Boys and girls were kept asunder.

I kept on dreaming, while she became a bride
A poet's fantasy remained unrealised!

Who was that lonely girl with luscious voice?
Living behind doors, bound by traditions
She hardly mixed with neighbours or friends
On rare occasions I saw her face, when
Light entered her netted windows,
Deprived of education, defeated by destiny
She obeyed silently her parents' dictates

And accepted her husband with rare grace.

While I watched, she left for an alien's home
A poet's remorse became a painful dream!

Who was she at the river's bank?
Dancing, twisting, and playing in waters
Swimming like a fish, and
Managing her costumes in teasing streams;
She spread the aura of youthful charm, and
Captured my sight like a magnet in action.

I kept on pondering - she met a partner
A reticent poet sent her flowers.

Where are those farms and dusty suburbs?
They were like cradles of childhood years,
Where are those friends and groups?
And those who played *Kabaddi* and Checkers,
Where are those groves and fruit-laden trees?
And the girls who sold mango juice in earthen glasses!

These reflections lie deep in a poet's perception
They travel along in the memory lane, and
Talk to me when I feel alone.
Had I possessed a camera
I would have captured their copies forever
And received some warmth today
When I am feeling the frosty cold of isolation.

6. My Shadow Talks

After a gruelling day in the office
I entered my home late in the evening
Tired, exhausted, and hungry
The weather was sultry, and mind sleepy
A time that needs cosy company
But the house was deserted and empty
It was the ugly face of twenty-first century.

Soon I encountered a full-sized mirror
My 'Self' came to life, greeted with 'Hi'
I jumped on my feet, surprised and bemused
Seeing my shadowy-self chatting with delight!
'Have tea or a glass of wine.
Relax, look inside.
I was always with you – like an intimate lover
But you seldom cared in life's vibrant hours
You were catching butterflies in pubs and clubs
And in friends' castles!'

The voice continued
'Life's journey is uncertain and long
You need someone to come along
Else, frustration can overpower your vision
And a beautiful creation ends without fruition.'

I grabbed a glass of grog
And relaxed on a sofa closed eyes
Wondering whether it was a ghostly illusion
Or a melodrama of unruly emotions,
Soon I felt a spell of lazy slumber
And saw a brunette emerge from nowhere
She smiled, came aside, touched my hair
And finally entered my physical structure.

I realised *beauty lies inside*
Never let it fade or dry
Poetry works like a manicure of mind
So, I venture to write these lines!

7. Search for Global God

In this age of globalisation
And as a member of the younger generation
I earnestly ponder
How to recite hymns in praise of God?
At a place of worship
Priests offer prayers from old scriptures
In a twisted combination of words
Often incomprehensible and borrowed as loans,
How can I meditate
When the place is agog with noisy rituals?
O Almighty, please pardon my silence
I can only salute you from a distance.

The West has entered my habits and manners
And English reigns over my daily fixtures,
How can I preserve the dictates of my culture?
Termites have already eaten my books
And Sanskrit is no longer within my easy grasp.

O Omniscient Lord,
I can't comprehend the meaning of verses
Spoken in Sanskrit
That seems an arduous test of my IQ,
Priests' words sound repetitive and insipid
Simply meant for earning a livelihood,
On tele screens you appear an actor
Cleverly used for minting money by film makers.

In a high-rise flat in a metropolis
I have no space for Lord Vishnu's statue
I wonder - how to perform my religious duty?
Taking a clue from my digital friends
I have saved His picture in my smartphone

And I listen to lyrics composed in His honour.

I grew up in Delhi, studied in London
Got married in Beijing and reside in Sydney
In my courtyard thrives
A complex web of Hindi, English and Mandarin
And my child has got entangled their-in.
O Lord, how can I pray in this linguistic confusion
I hardly know which language you prefer in this situation.
Also, I hesitate to explore my wife's feelings
While I am waiting to hear her heart's beatings.

I conquered the world on becoming a global citizen
And the global guru 'Google' has changed my vision,
O God, kindly do me the last favour
By showing your 'global form' at this juncture!

8. Cultural Garden

It was a bright sunny morning
Dew droplets on velvety grass were shinning
Children were playing, pushing, and shouting
A lovely sight worth watching,
Soon the bell rang
And they left for class with a bang.

The teacher looked grave but suave
After a cordial 'good morning'
He took them to the garden of global village
Through his words of a timely lesson.

You are the lovely birds of this cultural garden
Singing, chirping, roaming, and humming
Spreading fragrance here and there.
In your presence
White, black, brown and yellow mingle together
Like a cute painting on a clean paper,
The message is loud and clear
It's a nation of mixed cultures - why to fear?
You are like a multi-coloured flower
Bonded together with a sense of humour.

Only days ago, I had seen a large garden
Manicured, maintained, guarded by watchmen
But bored and frustrated, I left very soon
As all the flowers wore the same colour
Defying the nature's elegant selection.

A rainbow's beauty lies in its seven colours
Single colour would be devoid of glamour,
It's a lesson for all humans, and
Time is ripe for accepting nature's wisdom,

O boys and girls
Make it a part of your life's mission
That is expected of the younger generation.

You will see changes all around
That includes your fancy neighbourhood
You will meet people
With varied cultures, costumes, and manners
And Australia will change for the better.

Your presence is felt across the horizon
And the morning is waiting for a new vision,
You can create an oasis in desert's summer
And restore the glory of human endeavour,
You are the welcome prodigy of a 'lucky country'
And time has come to celebrate this journey.

9. Flight No. 2017

Working on a computer terminal
I booked Flight No 2017
The Airline's name was My-Dream
The destination was Milestone-2018
The departure date was 31 December 2017
The time was 24.00 hrs
The terminal number was Zero in Dreamland.

The computer was alert
It said, "24.00 hrs is not in my memory
Do you mean 00.00 hrs?"
"No, 00.00 hr means the beginning of a day
But I want to leave at the end of a day
Ask your supervisor to fix the problem
In the age of atomic clocks, one needs precision."
"Yes Sir, I will do
Now tell me about your baggage
How many kilograms?"
"Zero kilogram, and
Please write that on my ticket
Else, they will consider me travelling without baggage."

"Sir, I have never heard of such a baggage
What could be its contents?
Passengers like you are prized for the Airline
So, you deserve extra frequent flyer points."
"It is not my habit to divulge the contents
But I make an exception seeing your good manners
My baggage contains
Goodwill, love, and sweet memories
Which I could earn this year
And there is no balance to measure their weights,
I have left behind the heavy ones

Made of sorrow, jealousy, and painful moments."

After a cryptic silence for a few seconds
The computer came alive
"Though your contents are not listed in our database
Your baggage has been booked
With especial permission.
Now tell me: do you have a cabin bag?"
"Yes, I do."
"And its contents?" asked the computer.
"A few books, and some
Almonds, pistachios, and cashews for the year-long flight."
"Are you crazy? Or an author or a poet?
Books are the luggage of the past years
Now e-Books come in handy smartphones,
Carry a gift for your girlfriend or wife
That will certainly enliven your life."

Surprised, at the bold suggestion
I gave a short sermon
"Scholars are often digging for historical remains
One day they might dig up my books,
Who knows?
Computers may behave like crazy humans
And retrieve my books from the Clouds!"

"What about your return flight?"
"Yes, I will return by Flight No. 2018
Its date and time will be very similar
But as the world is sinister, and time is long
I cannot foresee the weight of my baggage,
God willing
It will remain Zero kilogram!"

A voice came from the computer
"Wish you a happy journey in the new year

May your resolution resound world over!"

(Theme: Lively fiction, glimpse of artificial intelligence, 'Clouds' refer to cloud computing; new year resolution)

10. Google's Kitchen

Hello, Hello!
Bob's kitchen? Can you hear me?
I would like to order a pizza.

Yes sir,
I can hear you very clearly
But it is no longer Bob's kitchen
It's Google's kitchen now.

What? Never heard of it.

Yes sir, you are right
Very few people know us
Google bought it only last week
Soon ads will appear on TV and Facebook.

Ok, please take my order now.

Sir,
Do you want the usual stuff?

What do mean by usual?
Do you know my taste? My choice?
Or my habits?

Sir,
It is the modern digital age
And Google is the master of AI
I am just a trainee robot …

What's this nonsense - AI?
Don't be cryptic with me
Else, I will complain to consumer affairs.

Sir,
AI means artificial intelligence
A product of ingenious human mind
But used by a computer's notorious brain.

Oh, I see
Then explain me your cryptic answer.

Sir,
Our caller ID database has saved
Your phone number, name, and home address
They match with your identity
And GPS indicates that you are at home.
Our past record shows
You ordered pizza more than a dozen times
And each time it was the same
With sausage, tasty cheese, and creamy sauce
Sprinkled with salt and chilli powder.
Do you want the same?

Yes, I do.

Sir,
We have your updated medical report
Your BP is high, cholesterol is raised
And you are over-weight by 20 kg at least.
Under Google's guidelines
Keeping you healthy is our concern
So, your choice shows a warning red signal
And I am duty-bound to reject your order.

What the hell?
Who gave you my medical records?
It is a serious breach of privacy
My attorney will sue you for conspiracy
You hardly deserve any mercy.

Sir, please calm down
No one can sue artificial intelligence
It has no physical entity like a human being.
I can take your order for a different pizza
Loaded with tomatoes, onions, broccoli
And a bit of roasted chicken for flavour.

But I hate seeing vegetables on my platter
I can't accept your nasty advice, and
Don't consider me a silly novice.
Also,
I take regular medicine for hypertension
So, there is no cause for any apprehension
Feed this information in your computer
And deliver my usual pizza without hesitation.

Sir, pardon me
My computer has accessed your local pharmacy
Three months ago
You had purchased 30 tablets for 60 dollars
One month's supply as per doctor's prescription.

How dare you question my integrity?
Can't I purchase from a different pharmacy?

Yes, you can
But it does not show on your credit card bills.

What a joke?
Where did you see my credit card bills?
Are you selling pizza or spying on the public?
What if I purchased by paying cash?
Does it not enter your silly brain?

Yes, you can

But during past three months
You haven't withdrawn more than 30 dollars
As shown in your bank statements.

I got some cash from my parents
Do you have any objection?

Fine, you are blessed
But that doesn't appear on your tax return.
I advise you to amend your tax return on time
Else, you may be charged for committing a crime.

You bastard,
How can you threaten me in this manner?
I have many friends in the upper echelon
Soon they will teach you a timely lesson.

Sir,
I apologize for my offending language
But kindly do me a favour
If your order is not completed within minutes
I will lose my bonus for the day.
Just for a change
Please accept my offer as a one-time test
I will add some extra pickles for your taste.

Ok, go ahead
And charge it on my credit card
The number is ...

Sir,
That number is alive on the monitor
And I have just pressed the charge button
The invoice will soon appear on your system.

How clever?

You know how to dupe a customer.

Sir,
Please keep cool and enjoy the dinner
Invite your girlfriend for a soothing atmosphere!

Thanks,
But before I let you go
Tell me if there is a Google's kitchen in Beijing
It is a modern city worth visiting.

Sir,
It is a million-dollar question
I am not allowed to answer in the open,
But before you book your flight
Don't forget to renew your expired passport.

Wow! Wonderful!
Omnipresent, omniscient, and what not
Just a step behind God's might!!

11. Digital Living

A jolly daughter wrote to her mother:
I am getting married soon this year
In a make-shift tent on Sydney's Bondi beach
And dinner is in a hotel near the iconic Opera House.
Please ask dad to save some money
I shall be flying from Beijing
With handcrafted costumes for the wedding.

Mom,
I met an antipodean on a dating website
Exchanged some photos on Facebook
Chatted for days on WhatsApp with little break,
Then he proposed to me on FaceTime, and
I agreed immediately with delight,
It was about a month ago
And now we are ready to go.

He belongs to a metropolis of the north
Located around latitude 40N
But I live 'Down Under' not far from 40S.
It is hot summer there, and cold winter here
So we have planned our honeymoon
In an equatorial region with congenial weather.

Mom,
Kindly do me a favour
Arrange a credit card for my endeavour
As a token of your blessings at this juncture
I promise to return it with lots of pleasure.

The mother replied:
I suggest you marry on Twitter
But before that you consult a cyber-expert

And confirm that your fiancé is not a robot
Or a notorious fraudster in disguise.
In future
If you encounter a problem
Sell your husband on Alibaba.com
And buy a new one on eBay.com

The daughter argued:
Mom, please don't be upset and angry
Accept the changes in life's journey,
When you were young
You went to church, listened to sermons
Made donations and returned with satisfaction.
As a member of the digital generation
I see human relations as a product for consumption
Give me a chance
This is an era of eventful experimentation.

12. Buy One, Get One Free

I saw a big ad in the morning
About a fancy store's event that evening
"Buy One, Get One Free" was very inviting
I could not resist, went for shopping.

The shirt was already marked down
And that too with a second one free
I grabbed one in a haste
Though it looked glossy for my age.

A few steps ahead
There was a bunch of hand-made silk ties
The delightful salesgirl chose a pair for me
I hardly needed but could not dare to decline.

Not far from there
I saw rows and rows of fancy suits
My temptation lost its bounds
I hesitated, but excused myself for once
And entered the fitting room for trial.

Before I could decide
The salesgirl packed two pairs, saying
"Blue and cream will suit on you."
Undecided, I asked for the price
She replied with a magical charm
"It's a bargain for the quality we deliver
Gentlemen like you never question my offer."
I was obliged to say "thank you"
And then, I walked away from there.

Before I could reach the elevator
A young guy came running after

"Sir, the suits you have bought are branded
So, they must have matching shoes."
A passer-by stopped, and nodded
I had no choice, but to curse the day!

When I saw the invoice at the counter
I felt a sudden headache
The shop assistant brought a glass of water
And got me seated on a cushy chair
Finding me stable, he whispered in my ears
"The brown shoes are made of soft leather
Use them for massaging your head
If the pain gets serious."

Before I could digest its meaning
He disappeared in the milieu
Even after six months
That invoice appears in my dreams and hurts
I wonder "How practical he was!"
A year after
When I saw the same advertisement
My heartbeat suddenly increased
Whether "to go or not" was a difficult question
It was like a mathematical equation
Where variables are 'wisdom and emotion'
Which has no credible solution.

Just then
I read the advice of an economist
"Do shopping without caring for money
This will increase gross domestic product
And ensure employment for all
Including your sons and daughters,
And above all
It will test your love for the nation
After all, we have to avoid recession!"

Before I could comprehend its meaning
A gust of fresh air blew over my head, and
I heard the dictum of Charvake's philosophy:
"yaavat jeevet sukham jeevet, rinam kritvaa ghritam peevet"
I became alert
It was a godly signal for doing shopping at best!

My footsteps followed the obvious course
I took my family and friends along
As we had to prove our loyalty to the nation!
In this era of twenty-first century
Charvake comes alive, looks larger than life
Proof lies in rising bankruptcy and credit card bills!

But don't be sad – have a hard drink
And start from the beginning again!!

(Context: A satire on material consumerism;
Charvake's philosophy: 'eat, drink, and be merry')

13. Where is Moonlight?

Where is full moon's silvery light?
And the wonderful glitter of this very night?
It is not me, but
A group of birds is asking this question
They have travelled far and wide
Without caring for thirst and hunger
Their eyes are tired, but
They haven't found that eternal light.
Who has stolen:
Their natural companion, and
The glow of Milky Way in the night-sky?

These are serious questions
Do we have their credible answer?
The smoke has swallowed the Moon, and
Moonlight is wrapped in a blackish costume
Shukla-Paksha has faced a defeat, and
Krishna-Paksha has turned victorious
Who will tell the birds: "This is our defeat."

Earth is also aggrieved
At the ugly face of the beautiful sky
She asks with remorse "Is this my fate?"
Who will tell her: "It's defeat of civilization!"

Whether we call it climate change
Or the vagary of growing pollution
It's man-made and harmful to lively creation,
There is an emerging opinion:
Preserving nature's sanctity is our new religion
When survival is at stake, we can't afford to be slack.

The blue planet is throbbing with life

Living in affinity with sisters in sky
Humans need to live in harmony
Or face the revenge of Nature's agony!

(*Shukla-Paksha*: the fortnight culminating in full moon,
Krishna-Paksha: the fortnight culminating in moonless night)

14. Death: A Perception

O god of death,
I know you will certainly come, then
Why not today?
Why not now?
The windows of my cabin are open
So are the windows of my heart and mind
I am alert and ready to welcome you
As you are a messenger of the merciful God.

Once I lie in the ICU, perhaps soon
You will come
But like a thief, unseen, unfelt
Of what benefit to me?
Or to your dignity?

I will salute you - if you save me
From the worthless needles
Digging into my veins
I have seen their felony
I can't bear that agony!!

Are you a dreadful black shadow?
Or are your costumes dirty?
I have heard
The God is sublime, source of divine light
And merciful at the most,
But I hardly see those traits in you
Though you claim to be a part of Him!

Are you the so-called god of death?
Or the heartless merchant of death?
I am waiting for your answer
And that will be my last dinner.

15. Poison of Corruption

This is Mr Ram-Krishna Shankar Chauhan
The special guest of a reputed hospital in the town,
While delivering a fiery election speech
His blood pressure had shot up
He lost his balance and collapsed on the podium
Unconscious like a person in deep slumber.

The whole country is grief-stricken
A doctors' team is engaged in his service
Anxious to diagnose and cure his ailment, and
Dreaming of a reward from the leader in future.

After numerous expensive tests
A subtle change in his DNA was detected
And its probable cause was *poison of corruption*
The team debated: 'What could be its remedy'

An expert physician asserted:
"It is a case of adverse *genetic mutation*
That can be treated through *genetic engineering*."
After deep contemplation
Another savvy consultant explained:
"If we can procure the DNA of *virtuous conduct*
That can be transplanted over the polluted section
And the leader's DNA will get purified in time.
If this experiment succeeds
One may expect the award of Nobel Prize!"

"Do you mean DNA of honesty?" quizzed someone
"Yes, in simple plain words
But it takes root through prolonged virtuous living."
All the experts wondered:
"Where and how can we get the DNA of honesty?"

The question was complex and puzzling
Its answer needed dialogue with other academics.

The next day, a noted sociologist suggested:
"We should find a *sadhu-mahatma* or *sanyasi*
Living in mountains - away from social pollutants
They eat vegetarian meals, and
Purify their inner-self through meditation and prayers,
The DNA of honesty would be present in their bodies
And that can be retrieved
If one gets a small bit of their blood, or skin, or hair."
"Agreed," came the unanimous approval.

After myriad attempts, one could get
A piece of black hair from an ascetic's beard
Which involved bribing his alert bodyguards!
The analytical result of that hair read:
"It has been corrupted by toxic hair-colours
So, its use is prohibited for genetic therapy."
Someone dared to say:
"It seems honesty got buried with our ancestors
So, the remains of their bodies would be precious."

Agents are looking into snowy Himalayan caves
For the frozen remains of the ancient *rishis*,
If they succeed
Experts can see the 'DNA of virtuous conduct'
And send its image to the national parliament!
Multinationals have also joined this race
Eager to patent the product using copious means!

In the meantime
I am bewildered at the paradoxical situation:
The leader's name flashes the image of holy gods
But his heart is the home of a dishonest deeds
I wonder if it's a phase of moral degeneration!

(**Hints:** A satire coupled with science fiction, DNA contains genetic instructions)

Other books by the author

In English:

1. Beyond Blue Oceans: One World One People
   Anthology of Poems, Paperback (2013) & eBook
2. Reflections: Poetry of Composite Culture
   Anthology of Poems, Paperback (2014) & eBook
3. One Face Two Minds: Living under Two Cultures
4. Short Stories, Fiction, Paperback (2016)

   Available from Amazon.com, Amazon.co.uk,
   Amazon.com.au, amazon.in

In Hindi:

1. Kavita Darpan
   Poetry (Hard Cover), Vani Prakashan (2013) New Delhi
2. Kshitij Ke Par (Across the Horizon)
   Short Stories, Fiction, Paperback (2014)
3. Kavita Kalash: Mirror of Cultural Interface
   Poetry, Paperback (2015)
4. Bolti Kahaniyan
   Short Stories, Fiction, Paperback (2015)
5. Kavita Saagar
   Poetry, Paperback (2017)

   No. 2 to 5 available from Amazon.com, Amazon.co.uk,
   Amazon.com.au, Amazon.in
   No.1 available from the publisher's website.

Made in the USA
Columbia, SC
08 September 2019